The Island of Ghosts

WINNER OF THE BISTO BOOK OF THE YEAR AWARD, 1990

'A rare treat ... The reader is kept turning page after page.'
THE IRISH TIMES

'(Eilís Dillon's) writing has always been distinguished by the
vividness of her imagination and her feeling for atmosphere.
This book is no exception.'
JUNIOR BOOKSHELF

Special Merit Award to The O'Brien Press
from Reading Association of Ireland
*'for exceptional care, skill and professionalism in
publishing, resulting in a consistently high standard in all
of the children's books published by The O'Brien Press'*

EILÍS DILLON was born in Galway in 1920 and died in Dublin in 1994. Her award-winning books for children and adults are internationally renowned.

Other Eilís Dillon books from The O'Brien Press:

The Five Hundred
The Lost Island
The Cruise of the Santa Maria
Living in Imperial Rome
The House on the Shore

Also by the Same Author:

The Seekers
Down in the World
The Shadow of Vesuvius
A Herd of Deer
The Seals
The Sea Wall
The Singing Cave
The Island of Horses
A Family of Foxes

THE ISLAND OF GHOSTS

EILÍS DILLON

THE O'BRIEN PRESS
DUBLIN

This edition published 2001 by The O'Brien Press Ltd.,
20 Victoria Road, Dublin 6, Ireland.
Tel: +353 1 4923333; Fax: +353 1 4922777
E-mail: books@obrien.ie
Website: www.obrien.ie

ISBN: 0-86278-708-4

1 2 3 4 5 6 7 8 9 10
01 02 03 04 05 06 07

The O'Brien Press receives
assistance from

The Arts Council
An Chomhairle Ealaíon

Editing, typesetting, layout and design:
The O'Brien Press Ltd.
Cover separations: C&A Print Services Ltd.
Printing: Cox & Wyman Ltd.

Chapter One

UNTIL THE TIME HAD ALMOST COME TO LEAVE OUR ISLAND, I had never thought much about what this would mean. Sometimes I would feel a shiver of excitement run through me, as if some strange marvellous thing was about to happen, and then I might pause for a second to wonder what my new life would be. But I was usually too busy to bother with it. Other people left to go to boarding school, as I meant to do, or to their uncles and aunts and cousins in Portland, Maine, or to find work in Dublin, if they were not needed at home. It was the natural thing.

Still I had often noticed that when they came back for a visit the returned emigrants were never quite the same, never really part of our lives as they had once been. No one made any remark about this. It was just something in the way the talk would stop for a second when they came into the room. I knew the reason – everyone felt that our little concerns couldn't be interesting to people who had travelled the world.

We should have known better. We had in our midst a man who had travelled more widely and done more things in his lifetime than any of us could ever hope to do, and yet he lived on our island quite happily for many years after he retired from his work as an engineer. His name was George Webb, and try as they would no one had ever been able to put Irish on that. A more foreign name couldn't be imagined. The closest they got was in the nickname they gave him – Bardal, which is the Irish for a drake. As everyone knows, a drake has webbed feet. He accepted the nickname and knew it came from affection, not from any disrespect.

Mr Webb lived a little beyond the village, in an old stone house that had once been the teacher's residence, before the new house near the school was built. He was not a tall man by our reckoning – we have very big men on the islands – but he was as wiry as the best of them and he handled the oars of a *currach* as if he had been born to it. He owned his own *currach*, which he had built himself. He also had a bigger boat with sails, of the type we call a *gleoiteog*. He and my father had raced her together in Kinvara several times and even though they won each time, they always seemed to have new plans for improving her.

Our island is Inishglass, and if you know your

geography you will remember that it lies two miles west of Inishrone, at the mouth of Galway Bay. Inishglass means the grey island, and that is how it seems from the mainland. When you look across from Carraroe, all you can see is a low shore covered with smooth rocks, rising gradually to a long grey rocky ridge. But beyond the ridge there are green valleys with good grazing land and fields where we grow our potatoes. There are three villages. The school is in Barna, the village closest to the pier. Because of the ridge behind it, it gets some shelter from the west winds that roar across with a noise like a squadron of aircraft for most of the year.

Our house was the nearest to the pier. My father was the postmaster, perhaps for that reason, and when I was small, before the helicopter began to come, my sister Barbara and I were always among the first to run down there on post days and watch the boat tie up. It's not much of a pier, just a short curve running a hundred yards out into the water. The boat always had to wait for the tide and the Captain made sure to skip out again as fast as he could, when he had delivered his bags of letters. I thought it very peculiar that mainlanders always seemed afraid of being stranded on an island. I know better now.

My name is Dara Faherty, and if you were to count the boys with that name on Inishglass at any time, you would easily reach the dozen. Most of them were my cousins, so we had to be distinguished by our parents' names as well as our own. I was Dara Thomáis, after my father. Dara is our saint, who lived in the sixth century. His stone hut is still to be seen, with its little well beside it, over on the shore opposite Barna. He is said to have known Saint Enda, who lived on the biggest Aran Island, and they used to meet once a year to pray together.

My greatest friend at that time was Brendan Conneeley. We were exactly the same age, and had always done everything together, ever since we walked to school for the first time and sat on the same bench singing out our a-b-c. Brendan had a young sister too, Cáit. The four of us played houses and shops as babies, and though the girls were kept closer to home than we were, we still called for them when we were going to the ridge after birds' eggs or wandering off to the Horses' Strand on fine summer days. Neither of them was allowed to go out in a boat, so we could never take them fishing, but they were always waiting to help us haul ashore when we got back to the strand with the *currach*. They went to our school too, of course, and sat together in the class below ours.

Our teacher was Mr Lennon, a decent good man, too quiet for his job. From time to time uproar would break out in the school, all the children running around and playing, throwing things at each other, laughing like a crowd of jackasses. This only happened when Mr Lennon had had a drop too much the night before and had a bad headache. Somehow we sensed his condition, someone would begin the game and in no time it was like a battlefield. Poor Mr Lennon would stand helplessly in front of us shaking his hands up and down like a seal, often finishing up by going out into the yard and sitting on the low wall, looking as if he were going to burst into tears. Then we would get sorry for him, and one of us would go out and lead him in, and promise to be good forever.

I suppose it was not easy to get a teacher to stay on the island, or he would certainly have lost his job. In fact he always said he liked it there, and he did what he could to prepare us for living in the outside world. That was what he called it, though I think he had never lived anywhere except Galway town.

Mr Lennon often said that the outside world was better if you got a scholarship and went to one of the boarding schools in Galway, or to the teacher-training college. Having seen the life that he led himself, I had decided that this last idea would not suit me.

Another prospect had presented itself through Mr Webb – his own profession of engineering. I was very quick at arithmetic when I was in the junior classes, and when I was twelve years old Mr Lennon let me join the small group to whom he taught algebra and geometry. This meant that I could try for a scholarship in two years' time, which seemed a lifetime to me then.

We had to go back after school for an hour every day and though the other boys laughed at us as they went off to help their fathers with the boats or on the land, I think they really envied us our status as special scholars.

I was running up the road to the schoolhouse for one of these lessons, one afternoon in September, when I met Mr Webb on his way down to our house to collect his letters. My father would have brought them to him but Mr Webb liked an excuse for a visit. On post days he would often stay an hour or two chatting, sitting on the hob by the fire while my mother or Barbara made tea for all of us and my father sorted the letters.

'Where are you off to?' he asked at once. 'Don't tell me you're going back to school.'

'Indeed I am,' I said proudly. 'I'm learning algebra now.' I loved that word. 'Mr Lennon said I can begin. I'm a bit late – excuse me –'

I made to pass him by but he held me back with a question:

'Why do you want to learn algebra?'

'It's like a game – I like working the things out –' I said.

'I just like it. And it's so easy.'

'Easy, is it? Well, you're quite right to like it. There's nothing like algebra. Bring me your book some day soon, and we'll talk about it.'

This was a splendid invitation but it was several weeks before I got up my courage to take advantage of it. Though Mr Webb rambled in and out of every house on the island, people rarely visited him. Children never did. There was something forbidding in the stiff, polite manner which he used to everyone. His house was set back from the road so that even though the door stood open, like every door on the island, you couldn't see right into the kitchen as you passed by. I had always thought the dark stone walls were in some way threatening. Our houses always glittered with whitewash. And the blank windows of the upstairs rooms, when the evening light glinted on them, were like spying eyes. If he had had a wife it might have been different, but with no woman in the house who would naturally welcome us, we were shy of intruding on him.

At last I knew I could put it off no longer. One Saturday, a wild day at the end of October, I was sitting by the fire in our kitchen, trying to make myself as small as possible. Even in the house we could hear the sea pounding on the shore, striking the breakwater to the back of the pier with ferocious force. When I looked out, I saw long jets of spray shooting up over the top, like dragons' heads.

Several men had come in, their wet boots making pools on the floor and seeming to take up twice their normal space. There they sat, puffing at their pipes so that the kitchen was full of smoke, and grumbling about the weather. The boats were all safe ashore and the cows and horses brought down near the houses. Even the donkeys were in their sheds. The men hated to be idle but on such a day there was nothing whatever to do. Outside our door the climbing rose-bush was battering off the last of its leaves against the house wall. When I said I would go out my mother said:

'God save us all – where would you go on a day like this?'

'I'll see what Brendan is doing.'

'Barbara is not going,' she said at once.

Barbara looked disappointed but she knew there was no hope of getting out today. I was sorry to leave her, listening to the voices getting lower and lower as the men began to talk about ghosts and fairies and disasters at sea. Always in bad weather some devil got into them and made them dredge up every gloomy story they could remember. You'd think they'd rather have had some music, or a bit of a dance, to cheer themselves up. As I slipped out of the house I heard Seán Black say:

'There's a queer story I heard only last week from a man I met in Galway, about the Island of Ghosts –'

Once they were on to that, there was no hope of stopping them. The Island of Ghosts is a small, windswept island, eight or nine miles to the north-west of Inishglass. No one had lived there for a long time, and the people of all the islands were never done making up stories about the spirits of the dead that inhabited it.

I slunk out of the house, followed closely by my sheepdog Bran. He was a small black-and-white collie, nearly my own age. No one could slink like Bran. He seemed almost to lie on the ground, until you saw that his legs were moving as fast as a fish's fins, sliding along beside you.

At Conneeley's house, I found that Brendan was sitting close by the back door looking as if he would love to dart outside. The wind was even stronger here, and every time it struck the end wall you thought it would blow it in. Brendan's mother said:

'Where did you spring from? Aren't you afraid you'll be carried off by the storm?'

'I'm going up to Bardal's house,' I said. 'I thought Brendan might come with me.'

'Do that, *a mhic*,' she said at once. 'I haven't seen him

all day. He couldn't put his nose outside the door today without having it whipped off.'

We were off before she could work out that if it was so dangerous for Mr Webb, it wouldn't be any better for us.

Brendan was the only one who knew why I was going. He was in the special class too, and of course I had told him of my invitation. Once we were away from his house, with the blown seagulls squalling above our heads like lost souls and Bran slithering along behind us, he held back saying:

'Maybe Bardal won't want to see me. He only asked you.'

'I wish you could come with me,' I said. 'I'm dying to go but I'm afraid of him all the same.'

'Why should you be afraid of him?'

'He's such a strange man. He looks at you as if he doesn't rightly see you. I'm thinking he'll only laugh at me.'

'Aren't you the best in the class already?'

'Maybe. Come with me a bit of the way.'

It took a few minutes of coaxing but at last he said:

'All right, just this time.'

As we reached the gate, we saw that Mr Webb was standing at the door, almost as if he were waiting for us. He came down the path a little way and called out:

'No dogs. I don't like dogs in the house.'

Bran crouched down, as he always did when he understood what had been said.

'I can't leave him outside,' I said. 'Anyway he's harmless. He's like a brother to me.'

'Very well, but he must be quiet. I see that you've brought Brendan along. Come in, both of you, and we'll get going. What better could you do on a day like this?'

That was how it started, and though Brendan was not at all pleased at first to find that he had school on Saturdays, he soon began to enjoy it as much as I did. We sat at the kitchen table, Mr Webb in a big chair at the head, with one of us at either side. You couldn't help enjoying it, though it was hard work too, and maddening at times. He had several books ready and he threw mine aside and began to show us problems out of his own. As soon as we had solved one, he produced another, then another, until at last he leaned back in his big chair and said:

'That's enough for today. Make sure you don't forget it all during the week. Pure knowledge, that's what algebra is, pure knowledge. But you'll see when you come to it that geometry is the queen of mathematics.'

Then he cut us each a piece of fruit-cake from a tin that he kept on the dresser. He even threw a piece of bread to Bran, who sloped out from under my chair to get it, then went back in again to chew silently.

It was on that first day that he began his discourse on Hy-Breasail, the mysterious island that very few have been able to find. We had heard of the place, but only as a sort of fairy-tale that the old story-tellers talked about. Now we found that Mr Webb believed in it very seriously, if not exactly as a real place, at least as an idea which could be realized by anyone with enough determination.

'Brendan,' he said, 'you should know all about Hy-Breasail. Your namesake, Saint Brendan the navigator, found it and described it in his writings. What do you know of him?'

'I've always heard he was a great sailor,' Brendan said, 'but I never met anyone who really believed in that island.'

'Perhaps they didn't understand what it means. Saint Brendan was more than a great sailor. He was an idealist. Mathematics, when you pursue the subject far enough, presents the ideal world, a world of order, a world under control. Some day the universe will respond to the challenge of mathematics and there will be peace among all men and nations. Can you see the logic of this?'

He was using words that we hardly knew, and we were not able to answer him. Neither of us would have dared to mention the name of God as the organizer of the universe. When everyone on the island gathered in the church for the priest's monthly visit, there was never a sign of Mr Webb. In our house he was prayed for every evening but it would have been rude to let him know about it. Fortunately he didn't expect us to answer his question. Soon afterwards he sent us off home saying:

'The details of what I teach you are important, but not as important as the concept of the total mathematician, the ordered mind that must be developed alongside the technician. Without that sense of order, all knowledge is useless. In fact it's dangerous.' On the doorstep he added:

'You can bring the dog next time.'

On the way home we talked about what he had said and tried to understand it.

'I thought I was only learning that stuff to get a scholarship,' Brendan said. 'He makes you start thinking about it in another way. He's spoiling it all, so he is, with his old talk.'

I didn't quite agree with that. I found that what he said had disturbed me, perhaps because he had shown me that there were a great many things in the world that I knew nothing about. One thing I discovered was that from then on I wouldn't miss those Saturday mornings for anything. Just sitting in the same room with Mr Webb was a lesson in something I couldn't name, as if he sent out rays of knowledge without using words at all.

Once, when my mother thanked him for the help he was giving us, he said:

'I like the company, and they work so hard it's well worth the trouble.'

Mr Lennon was the most pleased of all. He might have been jealous, since we soon began to know more than he did himself, but that was not his nature. When we reached the end of the first year he said we needn't come to his afternoon classes any more.

Chapter Two

IT WAS NOT LONG before we found out that one thing must never be mentioned in Mr Webb's hearing. We were both taken by surprise, since it was something that was simply a part of our lives. When it happened, he flew into such a rage that neither Brendan nor myself thought he would ever let us inside his house again.

The occasion was a simple one. As Inishglass is off the beaten track, certainly not on the flight line between Ireland and America, a huge jet plane passing over the island was a rare sight to us. It seems that in very good weather one of the pilots loved to change his route, so that the Aran islands and ours and the others along our coast would show in their full beauty, lying all green and silver like a page from an atlas, ringed with white surf in a deep-blue sea. Over his intercom he would tell the passengers to look out at the magic scene below. Down there, of course, we were looking up at him, and there was hardly a boy on the islands who didn't envy the people who were on their way to see the seven wonders of the world.

One gleaming sunny Saturday morning in the spring we heard the great plane coming. It was a quiet hum at first. We couldn't be sure of it until the heavy drone got louder, then our ear-drums seemed to beat in time with the huge engines. We looked at each other with delight, then without a word we leaped up and ran to the open door. There it came, its long plume following it like a tail, the sun shining on its silvery body, its green stripes clearly visible, seeming scarcely to move at all as it flew slowly closer and closer. Our heads were craned back so far that they felt as if they would break off, but still we stared upward, lost in another world, possessed by the magic of the powerful machine.

Suddenly we each felt a hard hand on our shoulders and we were wrenched in an about-turn and marched back into the house and the door was slammed with a sound like thunder. Brendan's face was white, and I'm sure mine was no better. I found my tongue first.

'What is it? What's the matter?'

I managed to force out the words, almost unable to look at his furious face. He gave a sigh, as if he had been holding in his breath, and turned back to his place at the table. Still we stood there, Brendan looking up under his lowered eyebrows as he always did when he was ready for a fight. I shook my head at him and got only a determined glare in reply. Mr Webb sat down heavily, not looking at us but at his hands, which lay on the table clutching each other so tightly that the skin on his knuckles showed white.

'How could you know?' he said at last, very softly. 'I'm sorry if I frightened you. How could you know?'

'What?' I said, as he didn't go on.

'Those terrible machines – those instruments of destruction and death –'

He stopped again and threw his hands apart, then let them fall lightly on the table. He glanced up at us suddenly and it would break your heart to see the look on his face.

'It's only a passenger plane on its way to New York,' I said, trying to give him some comfort. 'I'm sorry we ran outside. It's only that we don't see them that often. It's like a big bird, a beautiful bird, that's all. Surely you've seen them come over the islands before.'

Now that I thought about it, I realized that I had never seen him joining in the general wonder at the miracle over our heads. I suppose I imagined that it would be beneath him. It had never occurred to me that there might be anything more in it.

'Yes, of course, of course I've seen them,' he said, as if he were talking to himself, then more firmly: 'I don't mean anything personal, of course. You're good boys – this has nothing to do with you. Let's get back to work.'

Brendan looked up and I was glad to see that he was showing some sympathy with the tortured man at last. He came over quietly and sat opposite me at the table. The lesson went on as usual, except that when we made a silly mistake Mr Webb just corrected us gently and led us to the next point. At the end of the hour he went to the dresser to cut the usual piece of fruit-cake and with his back turned to us said:

'I must explain a little – as I said, it's nothing to do with you. I just can't bear those machines.' It seemed that he couldn't even bear to name them. After a pause he went on, very softly, so that we could hardly hear him, using words that he would never have normally used to two island boys:

'For a long time I loved them passionately. They were my whole existence, my whole life. I dreamed them. I stayed awake all night, many a time, working out improvements on their engines. When I made a discovery I was like Cortez, or Vasco da Gama, or Christopher Columbus. I would go around in a dream for days, half satisfied and half angry because I hadn't done more.

Then I'd go to work again as if there was a devil inside me.'

He stopped as suddenly as he had begun and looked at us directly for the first time.

'One of them killed my wife. Now do you see?'

'Yes,' I said, after a moment.

'It was a great new experiment. We were working on it together. She was an engineer too. She was flying it herself. She knew it was dangerous. We hadn't quite finished but one of us had to try it out.'

'Where?' I asked, almost afraid to speak.

'Off the coast of California. She went out and just never came back. Now – do you see?'

'Yes. I'm sorry.'

On the way home that day Brendan said:

'If the Concorde were to come over, I wouldn't go out to look at it. Did you ever think a man could be knocked sideways like that, at the sound of a plane?'

'We saw for ourselves what it did to him. That must be why he's here, when he could be living anywhere else in the world. Do you think the old people know all about him?'

'Maybe. I never heard them talk of that story he told us.'

'I'd say they don't know it.'

'Then we shouldn't tell it. If he wants to, he can tell it himself.'

We thought we would hear no more of it. Indeed we hoped we would not. Neither of us wanted to see that scene repeated. But he did talk a little, as time went on, when he went into one of his discourses on the uses of mathematics at the end of our lessons. I stored away everything he said about engineering but Brendan said airily:

'I'm going to need my knowledge for adding up the price of lambs and horses and cattle. I'm going to be a farmer.'

'Like your father before you?' Mr Webb smiled.

'No. He lives in the Stone Age. I'm going to have modern methods. I'm going to study chemistry and biology and animal husbandry at the university and have a big grassy farm somewhere in the midlands, maybe in Tipperary.'

'What do you know about Tipperary?'

'We learned it in school, in the geography class. Mr Lennon showed us pictures. He said he had been there once himself. You'd lose your mind looking at the smooth grass.'

'Was it Mr Lennon who told you about chemistry and biology and all that?'

Brendan paused to make sure that Mr Webb was not

laughing at him. Then he said:

'Yes. He said we have a poor way of living here. It's much better where the land is good.'

'And would you never come back?'

'Of course I would come back. I'd come and show them all what a bit of knowledge will do. Then I'd go home to my big grassy farm. I'd like to breed good horses. Mr Lennon says that Irish horses are the best in the world.'

I had been getting uneasy, without knowing why, but Mr Webb didn't seem displeased with this.

'I doubt if Mr Lennon has ever seen an Argentinian horse,' he said. 'But some of his advice is good. That's an excellent use to make of your education. Just don't despise the Stone Age. Here on Inishglass we're surrounded by stones.'

'I have nothing against stones,' Brendan said, 'but I mightn't want to spend the rest of my life with them. I'm going to travel the world first, like yourself, before I get that farm.'

In June of that year we sat for the scholarship examination. There were eight of us, and we were speeded on our way with the good wishes and prayers of the whole island. The examination was held in a big new school in Galway. We sailed over to Aran to catch the steamer to the mainland. Then we spent three long days writing papers on English and Irish and mathematics and history and geography.

Brendan and I stayed with an island woman named Mrs Folan, who had been at school with my mother. She and her husband and children lived in a house near the fish market, by the Spanish Arch, where the Corrib river comes rolling and galloping down to the sea. It was a good thing that we were with her, Galway seemed so huge and strange to us. The tall stone houses and the shops full of wonders would have been quite frightening, if we hadn't been able to go back to her for advice about how to behave in the city. We should never draw attention to ourselves by staring, she said, nor ask questions unless it was a matter of life and death, and we were never to give information about ourselves to strangers of any age. This must have made us seem a crowd of suspicious outlanders to the other boys and girls who were sitting the examinations. We scarcely spoke to any of them. Afterwards I was sorry, but by then it was too late.

When we came out after each paper we compared notes about our answers and kept copies of them to show to Mr Webb. We were delighted with ourselves when we saw that we had found the same solutions, until I said:

'Perhaps we're both wrong.'

But we knew we were not. Mr Webb had taught us how to check and cross-check everything, and he had also taught us how to handle an examination paper, how to read it carefully, how to divide our time between the various questions. We made use of this information in all our papers, not merely in the mathematical ones. We felt quite sure that he would be pleased with our performance when we reached home and told him what we had done.

So it turned out. He came over to Aran with my father to meet us from the steamer, sailing his own *gleoiteog*. Even while we were in the eating-house, before we set out for home, he was asking how we had fared, going over the papers and our answers with a pleased smile, quickly announcing:

'All correct. You were worth teaching, the two of you.'

'It looks as if we'll soon see the back of them,' my father said, puffing quietly on his pipe.

Though it sounded like a joke, I could see that the idea was painful to him. Still, as I said, we all knew that we would have to leave the island if we got those scholarships, and no one would wish to hold us back. Mr Webb was silently poring over the papers. At last he looked up and said calmly:

'Yes, it looks like that.'

All summer long we were as free as air, or as the birds

that wheel and circle over the island. It seemed that the sun shone from early morning until nightfall. I awoke every day to the sound of the hens and ducks clucking over their food at the front door, while my mother called out on a high, clear voice to the stragglers:

'Chook-chook-chook! Cush-cush-cush!'

Then she would come in and make my breakfast of porridge and soda-bread and butter. Soon I would have finished the few jobs that were my responsibility, feeding the calves and the little pigs, harnessing the donkey for his day's work, doing some weeding in the cabbage-garden. After that I would be off with Bran close behind me, to find Brendan for a day's enjoyment. This was always the way with the boys and girls who had worked so hard all winter, at school.

As often as possible we had Barbara and Cáit with us, though as I said they were not allowed the same freedom as we were. All four of us spent long hours sprawled on the grass in the sun, high on the windy ridge of the island, talking and laughing about anything and everything. Although we were much too old for it, we sometimes went down to the White Strand at low tide and built castles of the wet sand, with walls and battlements, and watched with delight when the incoming tide washed into their channels and moats. We made small nets and caught tiny shrimps in them, and cooked them over a fire of turf on the smooth stones that had been thrown up by winter storms at the top of the strand. When a shoal of mackerel came into the little harbour, we caught them in baskets and cleaned them in the stream that flowed down to the sea by our house, then broiled them, wrapped in ribbon-weed, on heated stones.

We were at this one day, all four of us sitting on our heels breathing in the heavenly, oily smell of the cooking fish, Bran edging closer and closer every minute, when we saw Mr Webb coming towards us. We hadn't seen much of him all summer. He was out in his boat a good deal, going and coming to Carraroe or Carna, he said, often staying away for several days together.

We jumped up respectfully and stood in a half-circle, shy of him as we always were, believing perhaps that he would find us silly in our childish occupation. Naturally Brendan and I knew him better than the girls did. Bran slid over to lick his boots, and he bent down to pat him. I said after a moment:

'Would you like some mackerel? They're nearly ready.'

'Of course I would. I see you're experts at cooking them.'

He sat on the grass, quite at home with us, and took his share of the fish, eating it off the seaweed with the help of his pocket knife. We used our fingers, as we always did, though I had a fine new knife that my father had given me as a reward for my year's work. Each of us gave a small piece of our share to Bran, who spent a long time licking his jaws afterwards. When he had finished Mr Webb said:

'You're experts at eating them too. Fingers were made before forks.' Then he asked casually: 'Any news of the examinations?'

'Not yet,' I said, 'but it won't be long now.'

I was rather put out at his talking about them on such a lovely afternoon, while we were enjoying our feast in good company. In the last few days I had begun to understand fully that winning one of those scholarships meant leaving my parents and especially leaving Cáit, who had always been my special friend. I knew that Brendan would be lonesome for Barbara too, in the same way.

'It won't be long,' I said again. 'We'll run and tell you about it, the moment we have news.'

Chapter Three

IN THE LAST WEEK OF AUGUST, the news came. My father was the first to hear it, since the telegram was tapped out to him as postmaster of the island. He came into the kitchen from his little office at dinner-time and sat in his usual place at the head of the table looking very gloomy. I had heard the machine working for a long time and had guessed what was going on. Now it seemed that all our work had been wasted. In a flash I began to work out how I would tell Mr Webb, and how I would apologize for having failed him so badly.

My father saw that I was watching him, and suddenly he shook himself like a sea-bird drying its feathers. Then he gave me a quick, comical look and said:

'Don't mind your old daddy. He never had sense. You have the first two scholarships, yourself and Brendan. Maureen Keenan and Michael Folan and Patsy Connor have smaller ones. I ought to be smiling. It's only that I don't want to see you going from me.'

Barbara had jumped up and was hugging me with joy, half cutting off my view of my father's face. With my arm around her I said:

'I'll only be going to Galway for a while. I'll be back for holidays and then I'll be home for good.'

But though the first part of this was true I knew that most of the boys and girls who went off to school made their living away from the island afterwards. How did I know that I would be different?

They were all watching me, my mother smiling now though she looked as sad as my father at first.

'You will of course, *a ghrá*,' she said. 'There will be plenty for you to do here when you're a grown man.'

'You don't believe that, but it's true,' I said, burying my hands in Barbara's long, dark hair as if she were a cat. 'I'd rather live here on Inishglass than anywhere in the whole wide world.'

'What do you know about the wide world?' my father asked jokingly, but pleased with what I had said all the same.

'Only what I've heard from Mr Lennon and from Bardal. I'll have to see a bit of it for myself but I think I know what I'll do in the end.'

I was doing more than just giving them comfort, though I knew they were not taking me seriously. They clearly thought I was too young to have judgement in such an important matter and they fully expected that as with everyone else the lure of the outside world would be too much for me. But already I felt that my own place was the one for me and that I wouldn't change my mind no matter how much I was tempted by city lights. I had seen them come home in their city suits and their heavy shoes, a bewildered look on their faces, happy for the first few days of their holidays, then becoming more and more dispirited as the day for their departure drew near and they realized what they had thrown away.

'God bless Bardal,' my mother said heartily. 'Eat up there now and let you run up and tell him the good news.'

'Can I go with him?' Barbara asked. 'We'll go first and tell Brendan, and we can all go to Bardal's house together.'

'Off you go,' my mother said. 'It's a great day for us all, to be sure. I must make a cake for the evening.'

We ran like a pair of redshanks to Brendan's house and poured out the good news. Like mine, his parents looked sad at first, then his father searched in his pockets and took out two tenpenny pieces, one for each of us.

'For sweets,' he said, 'but don't spend it all at once.'

We paid no heed to that advice. Mrs Kane, who owned the only shop on the island, added a contribution of her own. I could never make out how she could be so skinny, surrounded as she was by jars and boxes of chocolate and sweets and biscuits.

Our first stop after the shop was Mr Webb's house. It would be a great disappointment if he was not at home, since news like ours goes cold after a while. It also travels fast. We wanted to be quite certain that he heard it directly from ourselves.

We never knew these days whether or not he had gone out in his boat, since he no longer used the island quay. Instead he kept the *gleoiteog* in a cove below his house. This was a safe enough place in summer but a real death-trap in winter. From the equinox onwards, at the end of September, a wild west wind blew in there almost constantly, and it had such a bad record that even in summer the men were unwilling to use it in case of sudden storms.

When we came to the house we saw at once that he was there. The door was standing open and he was sitting at the table, studying a thick black notebook and marking it carefully as he read. When our shadows darkened the door he looked up quickly. One glance at our faces told him what had happened.

'Well,' he said calmly, 'I see you have good news.'

'The best,' I said. 'Both of us have won, thanks to you. We got the first two.'

'Your own work too,' he said. 'The old saying goes that you can't make a silk purse out of a sow's ear. Won't you bring the girls in?'

They came in shyly, since they had never been in his house before. He put his notebook down on the table, with the pencil between the leaves to mark his place. Soon he put the girls at ease, with plates of fruit-cake from his tin. He chatted while he was taking it out and cutting four slices for us, and a small one for Bran, saying that it was a special kind that came from Tuam, and that he always ordered it when he went to Carraroe. When he was sure that we were settled and at our ease he asked:

'So – when do you have to go?'

'In two weeks. The school opens on the tenth of September,' I said.

A sudden pain struck me through and through as I realized that I would not be here to see the long, amber sunsets and to hear the soft wash of the waves gently sending the seaweed drifting ashore. September was the best month for swimming, when the bladder-wrack released its juices into the water and made it soft as silk. Later, when the equinoctial gales came, there would be wild clouds scudding across the sky, warning the men to take in their boats, warning the seals to come in for shelter to the caves below the cliffs. There they would gather, singing their sad wailing songs which sounded so like human voices that the old people said they were the spirits of drowned sailors. And I would be far away in Galway, in exile from my land and my people as the old songs said.

Worst of all would be leaving Bran. Perhaps he wouldn't know me when I came back. Perhaps he would have become fonder of someone else, and wouldn't bother to trail after me wherever I went, as he did now. The thought of this turned a knife in my heart, so that I looked down at him where he lay at my feet, almost expecting him to have disappeared. He was there, all right, looking up at me at once with a sad face, as if he knew what we were talking about.

Mr Webb was watching me.

'You're not entirely happy to be leaving home,' he said quietly.

'Everyone must leave home sooner or later,' I said. 'We all know that.'

'Of course.' And then, for no reason that I could see, he began to talk about the Island of Ghosts. 'I've been out there several times,' he said. 'No one wants to talk about it. Do any of you know anything about it, or what was its story?'

'There was a family there long ago,' Cáit said. 'They were some way related to our family, I've heard. They all died and everyone says it has been an unlucky place ever since.'

'And the ghosts?'

'They say it's the ghosts of those people that walk there. My father said his father saw them once, a man and a woman, and he heard a child crying. He had gone in there for shelter and he had to spend the night on the island. My father said he was never willing to talk about it afterwards but he said no one should ever again set foot on it.'

'Never?'

'I suppose if there was dire necessity,' Brendan said, 'like a bad storm – then you would have to go in there, but the people around here would rather not do it.'

'Would you yourselves be afraid?'

'Those are old stories,' I said after a moment. 'The man probably heard the wind whining and thought it was a child, and his imagination would do the rest for him.'

'And you?' he asked Brendan.

'I never like to have anything to do with ghosts,' he said. 'How do I know where they came from? If they were up to any good, wouldn't they stay in the grave-yard?'

'But would you be afraid?'

'I couldn't answer that until I've tried it,' Brendan

said. 'I know that my grandfather was afraid of his life, and he had the reputation of being a sensible man.'

'There's beautiful grassland there,' Mr Webb said, 'fifty or sixty acres of it. Does no one even go over with sheep in the summer?'

'No. It's a kind of holy place,' I said. 'They wouldn't like to disturb the dead, even for the sake of the land.'

'As I told you, I've been there,' he said, smiling at our innocence. 'I didn't find anything ugly about it. It would be a wonderful place to live, like Hy-Breasail, where no one ever goes.'

'You can say that because you're a foreigner,' Barbara said. 'It would be different for one of us. Anyway, there's no such place as Hy-Breasail.'

Both she and Cáit had forgotten their shyness during the discussion. We could see that they liked Mr Webb as much as we did, now that they had come to know him a little, and like us they were specially pleased to hear someone talk freely about one of the taboo subjects on Inishglass. If we had tried to question any of the older people, even our parents, about the Island of Ghosts, we would have been told that curiosity killed the cat, and that it was no kind of talk for children. We had picked up what we knew here and there, from conversations that were supposed to be above our heads and in which we wouldn't dream of taking part. The people always used a low, tense tone of voice when they talked of such things, but I often thought this was silly and old-fashioned, and that anyway they only half believed their own stories.

On our way home Barbara said:

'It's no wonder you were always glad to go to him for lessons. I wish we could do the same.'

'I wish he wouldn't go on about the Island of Ghosts,' Brendan said uneasily. 'It's something we never talk about in our family. I don't think you should have told him the story about Grandad, Cáit.'

'What harm is it?' she said. 'Someone should have told him that story long ago. It's not as if he's a stranger. He's been living here for years.'

'People wouldn't like to know we took it on ourselves to tell him.'

'Then we won't say that we told him,' Barbara said. 'That's simple.'

I had been thinking about other things he had said.

'I wonder if he has told anyone else that he goes to the Island of Ghosts,' I said now. 'He didn't tell us to keep that to ourselves but I have a feeling that he wouldn't like it to be talked about.'

'It's none of our business to say anything about it,' Brendan said. 'He can talk about it himself if he wants to.

I don't want to have anything to do with that place. My father thinks that Bardal goes to Carraroe or Carna or Rosmuc. If he knew where he was going he mightn't be so friendly to him.'

So we decided it was an affair for older people, nothing to do with us. Then the excitement of the great changes to come put it all out of our heads. New clothes were to be bought for us. Our measurements were sent to Galway and parcels came back containing shirts and underwear and smooth, factory-made jerseys that would have stood no battle if we had worn them at home. We each had a suit for Sundays, and a tie, which we practised putting on in secret so as not to look foolish when the time came to show off our finery. The same was going on in the houses of the other scholarship-winners, you may be sure, and when we met all our talk was of the strangeness of it.

Now and then we went to visit Mr Webb but as often as not his door was closed and his boat gone from the cove.

'He doesn't care about us any more,' Brendan said when this had happened several times in succession. 'He's finished with us. We needn't bother coming again.'

'We don't know,' I said. 'It would look like very bad manners out of us if we were to stop coming to see him just because we got what we wanted.'

'That's true. Maybe he'll come down to the house

some evening to see your father,' Brendan said.

We had to be content with that. He did come a few evenings later, and sat quietly by the fire chatting as he always did. My mother fussed over a special pot of tea for him, and cut him slices of currant bread to eat with it, thanking him over and over for the help he had given me. He smiled and said, as he had said to us:

'It was really their own work that did it for them. It was a pleasure to teach them.'

We were well into September by now and there was a clear sharpness in the air. The evenings were shorter. By seven o'clock dusk had fallen and with no light for outside work the people began to drop in on each other for a visit.

Our house was a very popular one because the news was always fresher than any you could get on the radio. My father's official position made him important too, and it was known that he wrote a good letter when necessary, on almost any subject. This had given him a reputation for wisdom which he often found very funny, though he wouldn't have said so to the people who consulted him.

On my last Sunday at home, naturally a great many of our neighbours called in to wish me well. Some brought presents. Nellie MacDonagh, our next-door neighbour, brought a pair of socks that she had knitted herself, guaranteed to keep out the cold in the big house where I would live, and where she had heard there was never a turf fire that you could sit at to warm yourself. Colie Joyce, one of my father's fishing companions, brought a strong pocket-knife that he said would last me for the rest of my life if I took proper care of it. I need hardly say that I didn't mention the one that my father had given me already. Kate Folan brought a pair of pyjamas, so clean and beautiful in their box that I couldn't imagine ever wearing them.

After a while I found that all this attention was more frightening than pleasant. I could see from the way they looked at me that they expected a great deal from me, and I was naturally afraid that I would never be able to live up to this.

'It's the same with me,' Brendan said when I told him of my fears. 'You'd think I'd gone to the moon with the astronauts, or discovered the source of the Nile or something. I wish we were away and gone from the whole lot of them.'

Brendan always had less patience with people than I had but in this case I agreed with him. The girls had had to go back to school, but every chance we had, we were off together on the Ridge or to the wild coves on the western shore, below Mr Webb's house. It was there, on a

glowing afternoon three days before we were to leave for
Galway, that we found out at last what he was planning.

Chapter Four

HE WAS COMING DOWN the narrow gully that led to the strand, walking very slowly. From our position on the rocks above him we could hear his footsteps, heavily placed, as if he were carrying something big. We had been lying for an hour or so on the thin grass, enjoying the sunshine, but in the last few minutes we were beginning to feel the nip of a cold little breeze from the north-west.

I put my hand on Bran's neck to keep him still. We eased forward gently and peered over the top, making no sound, still unaware of who the visitor was. We might not have been surprised to find that it was Mr Webb, since we could see his boat moored to the rocky wall of the cove, but the shock of what he was doing made me call out before I could stop myself:

'He's moving his furniture.'

'Quiet,' Brendan whispered. 'Don't let him hear you.'

Bran had become very fond of Bardal, and at any moment he might have burst out with welcoming barks.

I clutched him by one ear and whispered to him to be quiet. Mr Webb was too busy to hear us, however, and the noise he was making would have covered all other sounds, including the little squeaks that the dog was giving now. He was carrying the lower part of his kitchen dresser, lifting it and placing it down carefully a few yards at a time, keeping his foothold with difficulty on the rolling, rough gravel, pausing now and then to stretch his arms, as if they hurt him.

'Come on,' I said. 'There's no point in being quiet. He'll kill himself if we don't go down and help him.'

'Maybe he doesn't want help,' Brendan said, but he followed me all the same.

We climbed down the sloping side of the gully, sliding the last couple of yards to the ground. Bran was well ahead of us, jumping around and barking with delight. Mr Webb looked far from pleased to see us – in fact he glared at us so angrily that I felt like climbing up the rock-face again and leaving him to deal with his own troubles. Instead I said:

'Why didn't you call for us? We would have come and helped you with that.'

He sucked in his breath through his teeth and said with a great effort at politeness:

'Yes, I'm sure you would. But I didn't want the whole

population to know what I'm doing.'

'Why not?' Brendan asked.

'Because it's none of their business. Now that you're here I'll be glad of your help. I was going to ask you to help me later, with some of the things. You haven't been to see me for a while.'

'Yes, we have, but you haven't been there.'

'Well, I was busy.' My answer seemed to please him. He sounded more friendly as he went on: 'Now that you're here, you can take a hand with this.'

'Where do you want it?'

'In the boat, of course. I'm moving house.'

We could see now that other things were already loaded into the *gleoiteog*. Several pieces of furniture were stored neatly in her, chairs and a small table and his bigger bookcase. She was floating nicely on the half-tide. Too much delay would leave her high and dry, and he would have to wait for the next tide to get her off.

'Does it surprise you so much that I'm moving house?' he asked impatiently.

'Of course it does.'

No one on Inishglass moved house. A house was where you were born, and where you stayed for the whole of your life, unless you emigrated or moved in with a family that had a house already, as some people did when they married.

'But where? Where are you going? To Carraroe? Or Galway?'

'I'm going to the Island of Ghosts,' he said, watching us with an expression I couldn't understand. 'I've told you, it's a good place. I've been to it often. No one lives there. It seems to me that I have as much right to be there as anyone. What do you say, Brendan? It belonged to your family once, I think.'

'Not exactly to my family – to some cousins. None of them would live there, as we told you.'

'And would they object to my living there?'

'I suppose they own it still,' he said doubtfully. 'But they're all gone from here long ago.'

'Where? Where have they gone?'

'Chicago. New York. They never come home. I've never seen any of them.'

'In that case I needn't worry,' he said with great satisfaction. 'But there's no point in telling anyone what I'm going to do. Is there?'

He shot the question at us so sharply that we stuttered our answers:

'No – no – no point – no point at all –'

'Then let's get on with the work.'

We lifted the piece of furniture between us and carried it down the slope to the boat. Mr Webb jumped in and eased it into position. Now we saw that he had already got the upper section of the dresser, the part with the shelves, in there too. We could see several cardboard boxes full of objects rolled in newspaper – his cups and saucers, probably, that used to stand on the dresser shelves as they did in every house on the island. Somehow that brought it home to me that he was really leaving.

'Is this your first load?' I asked.

'The first load of furniture, yes,' he said, 'but I've been working on a place to put my things for quite a while.'

A house, of course. He would have to have a house. So far as I knew there was none on the Island of Ghosts.

'There was a ruin,' he said, as if he were reading my thoughts. 'I've been repairing it all summer. It's weatherproof now. The walls were sound but the roof was almost gone. It must have been thatched – I've done it with slates.'

'Yourself? All alone?'

'Oh, yes. I'm used to fending for myself, though I would have used a helper if one had come along.'

'You could have asked us,' Brendan said.

'Could I? Well, perhaps I will next time.'

'We won't be here.'

'Before you go, then. Would you help me to take out my last load when the time comes?'

'Of course.'

'On one condition, though. You must not tell anyone where you're going.'

'That won't be so easy.'

'We're often out for a whole day,' Brendan said quickly. From holding back at first, he now seemed to feel that I was being churlish in not agreeing at once. 'The only trouble is that we have so few days left.'

'Tomorrow, in that case,' Mr Webb said. 'I'll take this load out myself now, and in the morning you can help me with the rest of the things. There's not much left. I must go now, or I'll miss the tide.'

While he was talking, he was busy hauling up sail so that the *gleoiteog* was straining on her ropes. We cast off for him and she leaped away from the rock in one beautiful movement, perfectly balanced with her cargo. When he was a hundred feet offshore he called out to us:

'Come early! We'll need the whole day for the work we have to do.'

'We'll be early,' we shouted back. 'A safe journey to you!'

He waved once, then set himself to managing his

boat. As we walked back up the gully Brendan said:

'Man, he's a fine sailor, and he has a sweet boat.'

'That's a queer plan of his,' I said. 'Imagine living alone out on the Island of Ghosts. He must be crazy.'

'Independent, I suppose,' Brendan said. 'You'd have to admire him for that, in a way. One thing sure, I wouldn't like to spend as much as one night on that island, not to mind the rest of my life.'

'Is it true that the land is good there?'

'Good enough, my father says,' Brendan said slowly. 'But he said there's a salt wind blowing over it for too much of the year and the sheep get sick if they're left there. He said that only for the wind they'd bring sheep out there all summer, and no one would take any notice of the old stories. I heard my father saying that you couldn't even keep goats there, it's so unhealthy, and goats are as tough as donkeys.'

'Do you believe that?'

'I don't, and that's the truth. I think it's the ghosts that keep them off. Land is land, no matter where it is. How could it be worse than Aran, or Inishglass for that matter? I'd swear that cattle would do well there, and seed potatoes too, and even a bit of oats. I think it was a good place in its day. But who would want to live with ghosts?'

'When was your father talking about it? Do you think

he knows what Bardal is planning?'

'Not at all. This was a long time ago, a year or more. I'm sure he doesn't know. I didn't talk about it at home, if that's what you're thinking.'

'Neither did I,' I said. 'He's a queer, silent man, Bardal, and if this is the way he wants it, we'll just have to fall in with him. The people that were nice to him will be sad to have him go without a word to them.'

I was thinking specially about my mother, who had always entertained him like a king when he came to our house, and made sure to take him fresh bread and soup if he got a cold. She had stood up for him when anyone said something against him, or talked about his strange, cold ways.

'They all know he's a bit of an oddity,' Brendan said. 'I don't think anyone will be surprised.'

What we didn't want to say was that we were hurt too. We had thought of him as our friend, and he seemed to have proved it by all the teaching he had given us and by his pleasure in our success. How then was he able to sail off and leave us without a word? If we hadn't chanced on him, we wouldn't even have known where he had gone.

'Anyway,' I said at last, 'the least we can do is to help him with his bits of things tomorrow. We can say we're going swimming at the Horses' Strand. That's what we were planning to do. It's going to be another fine day, by the looks of it.'

This somehow salved our consciences. It was true that we had talked of swimming the next day from the strand at the far end of the island. In our last days, we had felt that we must visit the places where we had played all our lives, and make sure that they hadn't changed. We knew that we couldn't possibly tell the truth. To reveal what Mr Webb was planning would have seemed to us the worst deception of all.

I was up and about so early next morning that my mother said as she came in from feeding the hens:

'You must be practising for school. I hear they get up at seven o'clock there. Eat plenty now, and you can take the rest of the bread with you for after your swim. And be careful not to go out too far. There's a nasty current around the rocks in September. Here, take a bit of bread for Bran. He'll be going in for a swim too, you may be sure. I can tell by the carry-on of him.'

By the time I reached Brendan's house I was in a state of panic. Never before had I remained silent in this way about my doings. It was bound to bring bad luck. Then, to make things worse, I saw Brendan's aunt, Nellie Mór, sitting on the big rock outside the door. This was her favourite spot on a fine day, though she was not usually there so early. She was a widow, and she had lived with Brendan's family as long as I could remember. For the last few weeks she had been away in Carna visiting her daughter and I hadn't heard that she was home.

Nellie Mór had the sharpest tongue on the island, and that's saying a great deal. She seemed to hear everything even before it happened, either from one of her friends or from a child who was passing by, or from some things she overheard and put together in her lively brain afterwards. It was because of her that I rarely spent more than a few minutes in Brendan's house, though he often came for half a day to mine. When we would be talking quietly to each other in the corner, she would put her head in between us to hear what we were saying. She kept a close watch on Cáit too, and was often the cause of her being kept at home when we wanted her to come out with us.

'Boys and girls shouldn't play together,' she would say, giving us a strange look. 'It's not natural.'

Nellie Mór was a huge woman, as her name tells. She sat on the rock as if she were carved out of it. She gave me a long, considering look and then said:

'Here comes the other scholar. I hear you're off to Galway any minute.'

'Yes,' I said loudly, hoping Brendan would hear me and come to my rescue.

'And you're going for a swim, I heard, to the Horses' Strand.'

'Yes.'

'And what's wrong with the White Strand all of a sudden?'

'Nothing, I suppose.'

'Some great attraction at the other end, that's dragging you all that way in the heat of the sun?'

'It's not very hot.'

'No, but you will be by the time you get there. Maybe the water-snakes will eat the pair of ye. But sure, ye'll have the big fierce dog to mind ye.'

By water-snakes she meant the conger eels, but I knew it was too late in the year for them. I made no answer, and just then Brendan came running out of the house, carrying his bag of bread. He grabbed my arm and pulled me away, calling out:

'Good-bye, Aunt Nellie! We'll be back in the evening!'

We ran up the hill and away from the quay, followed by her cackling laughter. After a while we slowed down and I asked:

'When did she come back?'

'Last night. She guesses there's something going on. If you stayed a minute longer she'd have your story out of you somehow.'

'I wasn't going to tell her anything,' I protested.

'Oh, yes, you were, but you don't know it. Come on, now, while we can.'

Bardal's door was shut when we reached it and the sun was blinding the windows. He opened to our knock at once and said:

'Come in quickly. Did anyone see you coming?'

'I don't think so,' Brendan said, 'but it wouldn't matter if they did. We said we're going swimming to the Horses' Strand. It would be natural to call in to see you first.'

'Good, good. I've taken down one load already. Now just help me with these last things.'

He was simmering with excitement, far worse than we were. While we loaded up with his settle-bed he kept dancing around us, giving us various pieces of advice, until I said at last:

'Just let us get the balance ourselves. We've often carried a currach in and out of the water. It will be much the same.'

'Of course.'

He was quieter then but even as he filled a cardboard box with sheets and towels, he kept turning quickly to look at us as if he thought we might have disappeared. I felt very sorry for him, setting out to live that lonely life. It was a great day for him, I told myself, much worse than for us. I certainly couldn't understand why he should do such a thing, and I didn't like the way he was watching us, but this was not very different from his usual way.

He led the way to the shore, carrying the box, while we followed with the settle on our shoulders. Bran kept running back and forth beside us, as if he knew that something strange was happening. The going was not too difficult, once we had climbed down the steep incline from the field at the back of the house. Being the taller, I went in front and took most of the weight. As we reached the cove I said:

'I don't know how you managed with the rest of the things, on your own.'

'Neither do I. Determination will do a great deal for you,' he said.

His mood had changed and he was whistling cheerfully as he helped to ease the furniture down into the boat. He must have been up since the dawn. His bed took up a large part of the space. Bags and boxes filled the rest of it, so that he had to climb over them to reach the sheets and haul up sail. I began to see that it was going to take a long time to unload all of these things when we reached the island. Then he would have to take us home, and sail back by himself.

I lifted Bran in my arms and placed him quietly among

some boxes in the stern, telling him to keep quiet. He lay down at once and put his nose between his paws. I knew from experience that a great many people don't want a dog in their boat, unless he's going to work with sheep. Sure enough, just as we were about to cast off, Mr Webb turned suddenly and asked:

'Where is the dog?'

'He's here, lying down quietly.'

'Get him off,' he said roughly. 'He'll have to wait for you.'

'Why?'

'He'll cause trouble. Put him off, I said.'

'But he comes everywhere with me.'

Then I realized that it was no use protesting. I could almost hear my mother's voice saying, 'Couldn't you have humoured the poor man when he was set on leaving the dog behind? Where did you leave your manners?'

I lifted poor Bran, who hung as if he were half-dead from my hands, and pushed him on to the rocks. There he stood, gazing after us, with the saddest face that ever a dog could make.

Judging by the sun it was already eleven o'clock when we cast off and slid out of the cove, slowly because of our heavy cargo and because the wind had dropped without warning almost to nothing.

Once outside the cove we made better speed. Then Mr Webb looked at us with a happy smile and said:

'Now, at last, we're off to Hy-Breasail.'

Chapter Five

IT SEEMED INDEED A MAGIC ISLAND, as we approached it from the sea. It had been a slow journey, with barely enough wind to carry us along. The sea was calm and shining, like a polished pewter plate. At first all we could see was a low shoreline with flat rocks, flowing upward gently to a long stretch of grassy land, and finally to a small peak like a lookout post. The island hung in a golden haze of mist, so that it looked as if it were floating above the surface of the sea.

On the lee side there was no sign of a harbour or cove in which we could make landfall with the *gleoiteog*, though the strand would have been fine for a *currach*.

'We have to go around to the west side,' Mr Webb said when we asked him about this. 'You'll see, there is a nice little natural harbour.'

'It can't be too safe on the west side,' I said. 'Surely the first storm will blow the boat to bits.'

'You'll see,' he said again.

The western side of the island, facing the broad Atlantic Ocean, was ringed with tall cliffs as steep as any on the Aran Islands. But sure enough, presently the cliffs gave way to a jumble of enormous rocks, and we steered between them into a sort of pool. Behind us the rocks had been worn smooth by the ferocious storms that lash that coast every winter, but we were suddenly in shelter. The light wind was just enough to take us in, and with the sails flapping eased our way along until we came to a new iron ring set in the rock with cement. Mr Webb jumped ashore like a monkey, a rope in his hand, and had us tied up in two shakes.

'There you are,' he said, 'made to measure.'

'What happens when the tide goes out?'

'It comes in again.' He laughed happily. 'We must unload first, and then you can come along and see the rest of my kingdom.'

We climbed in and out many times, scrambling over the rocks to the grass above, until we had all of the cargo piled up there. Then, carrying a few of the lighter things, we started towards what looked like a grey ruin some distance away. As we came closer we could see it was the gable of a stone house, with a huddle of stunted bushes in front of it, nestling under the shelter of the peak. A low wall surrounded a little garden in front.

The house had been neatly slated and the gaps between the stones pointed with cement. Its gable end was set to shelter it from the prevailing west wind. Its three windows, looking into the garden, were newly puttied and painted, and there were new stone sills on all of them. The area around the door had been paved with flat slabs of rock and the door itself was new, with a heavy brass knob. Stacked against the far gable we could see a clamp of good black turf.

'Where did the turf come from?' Brendan asked at once. 'Did you bring all that over from Connemara?'

'I cut it and saved it myself last year. There's a bank of turf up towards the peak.'

That surprised us more than anything else, since turf doesn't grow at all on the other islands. Indeed as we well knew from infancy, having to buy all their turf was one of the biggest worries of our parents, until the Government sent us bottled gas.

'And the work you've done on the house!'

The door was not locked. He turned the knob, watching us with delight, and led us inside. There were four rooms instead of the usual three. The bedrooms opened off either side of a central kitchen, which would also be the family living-room. Immediately he began to point out the best features of the building, the new rafters of heavy timber, the stone fireplace with its crane for carrying pots and its two hobs where one could sit close to the blaze in cold weather. He was specially proud of the little hot-water boiler that he had put behind the fire, with pipes leading to a sink and to two tiny bathrooms which he had built, off the bedrooms. He had also devised a way of sending the heat through ducts into the bedrooms so that they would always be warm and comfortable.

He was obviously very pleased with our praise.

'I'm not an engineer for nothing,' he said. 'And I'm a good stonemason and plumber too. Wait till you see my water-pump and the place where I'm going to put my generator. There's a splendid stream with a little waterfall. I had to improve that somewhat. I'll make a reservoir later, higher up. Come along and I'll show you.'

He made for the door, but I said:

'Shouldn't we get the things into the house first?'

The day was passing and a little wind had come up. I could hear it soughing around the corner of the house. By the time we had everything in place it would be afternoon, and he would still have two journeys to make if he intended to spend the night here on the Island of Ghosts.

'Very well,' he said, giving me a strange, almost inimical look.

I wondered if I had seemed rude in cutting him off but surely he couldn't have thought so. I had been thinking of him as much as of ourselves. I said nothing, however, and we followed him outside. At my ear Brendan said:

'He's like a cat with kittens. I never knew anyone so touchy.'

'Let's humour him,' I said. 'He has every right to be proud of this place.'

For an hour or more we lifted furniture and boxes and carried them up to the house. As we worked, we kept on discovering new things that he had been doing. He had rebuilt and extended a tumbledown shed at the back of the house and his tools were stored there, including the mallet and chisel for all the stone-cutting he had done, and a range of plumber's and carpenter's tools. In the same shed he had several sacks of meal and flour, some bales of straw, and a sack of oats.

'Who is going to eat the oats?' I asked in a daze, overwhelmed at all this foresight.

'Wait – just wait till you see.' He gave a little crowing laugh. 'There's plenty more to come.' He opened the door at the far end of the shed and disclosed a tiny section set up as a hen-house, with a dozen or so hens picking over the straw on the floor. There was a row of nesting-boxes along one wall and a stout red hen was sitting on a nest, hatching, glaring at us suspiciously. 'The chickens should appear any day now. I got the clutch from a woman in Carna.'

'You've thought of everything,' Brendan said. 'What about milk?'

'Goats and sheep. Come along.'

We followed him outside, almost having to run to keep up with him. He led us around by the back of the house, past the clamp of turf, into a walled field with a five-barred gate. Like all the islanders, the people who had lived here long ago had fenced their fields with loose stone walls. They are everlasting, and when they are built well enough they make a perfect defence against every animal except the donkeys. These are often clever enough to knock the wall down stone by stone with their noses, until they have made a gap through which they can escape.

There were four goats and several kids in the field, as well as a billy-goat. Beyond the walls, grazing free, we could see a little flock of sheep, a dozen or so, and two donkeys.

'My father said you couldn't keep animals here,' Brendan said in bewilderment.

'Did he, now?' Mr Webb chuckled. 'I'd like to see his face if he were ever to come here.'

'How long have you had them?'

'Two years this September.'

'And they don't get sick?'

'Never. At least they have never complained to me. Now I've really surprised you. There's more to come.'

Again he ran ahead of us. The sky was darkening and I could see heavy clouds moving in from the Atlantic. There was no mistaking the sharp edge on the wind, nor the little whistle that had come into it in the last half-hour. I called after him:

'Mr Webb! We can't stop to see any more. It will have to wait! We must get back – there's going to be a storm!'

He paid no attention to me, just continued on his way so that we had to follow. Brendan said as he ran beside me:

'He's out of his mind. I never thought anything like this would happen. They'll be in a terrible state at home if we don't get back before the storm comes on. They'll think we're drowned.'

'And I don't want to spend a night on this island if I can help it.' I was remembering the sad story of the family that died here, and the child that could still be heard crying. 'As soon as we've seen his next wonder, we'll have to tell him to take us home at once and no more nonsense about it.'

A little farther uphill he waited for us, where a spring welled up and ran off in a broad stream towards the sea. The well had been roofed with a stone slab, now covered thickly with moss, showing that it was the work of that long-ago family. Just where the stream began to fall downhill, a single hawthorn tree pointed spiky arms at the darkening sky, its haws gleaming in the pale sunlight like tiny lamps. Brambles and blackthorns grew there too, and the grass was lush and heavy from the well-water.

Before we reached him he was calling out:

'Here's where I'm going to put my generator, and make my own electricity. For the moment I have to use lamps. I've already piped off the water to the house, and I've buried the pipes so as not to spoil the look of the place. And I'm going to build an irrigation system for dry summers, and for watering the animals.'

Only a slight unevenness in the ground showed where he had carefully lifted the turf to lay the line of pipes, and then restored it all neatly.

'Mr Webb,' I said, trying hard not to sound impatient, 'there's a massive storm coming up. We must get back home as quickly as possible. If we delay any longer, we won't be able to go at all.'

He gazed from one of us to the other with a strange

smile. His blank eyes were like a goat's eyes. I couldn't make out what he was thinking but a shaft of fear shot through me, leaving me without a word to say.

'You won't be able to go at all,' he said after what seemed an age. 'That is true.'

'Then let's get down to the boat quickly,' Brendan said. 'Even ten minutes' delay might be too much.'

'It's too late already,' he said. 'Don't you know that?'

'No,' Brendan shouted. 'What do you mean?'

'Haven't you guessed? You're not going home any more. You're staying here with me.'

Even Brendan was speechless at this. Mr Webb smiled at us for a second or two, then turned away and began to walk back towards the house.

We looked at each other helplessly. Brendan tapped his forehead to indicate that he thought Mr Webb had lost his reason. At the same moment I put my finger on my lips, to say that we should be quiet. Then, with one accord and no need for any more sign-language, we bounded off down the hill towards the cove where the boat was moored.

Half-way there I turned quickly and saw that Mr Webb was watching us and I felt a momentary pang at the idea of leaving him. But no doubt entered my mind that we would have to go.

Brendan hadn't looked back at all. Though he was smaller than me, he could always run faster. He reached the cove a little ahead of me and stood, staring down into the boat.

She was floating free on the high tide, like a swan for ease and balance. Outside the cove the sea was a greenish grey, with white-capped waves and blown spume making a mist over them. The north-west wind would take us home quickly, as I knew very well, and she was a lovely boat. I couldn't make out why Brendan hadn't leaped down into her at once, and begun to haul up sail.

Then I saw the reason. Her rudder was gone. Idiotically, I looked around where we were standing, and over to where we had piled up the things we had brought from Inishglass, as if I might see that all-important piece of timber lying on the grass near us. It was all quite bare.

'He's taken it out,' Brendan said furiously. 'No wonder he didn't bother to follow us. He's taken out the rudder and hidden it somewhere, while we were foolishly packing away his property in the house. We'll have to go back and force him to tell us where it is. He'll have to give it up – he'll have to –'

We looked out at the open sea, which in those few moments had become still more threatening. Even for experienced sailors, it would have been impossible to take the *gleoiteog* out of the cove without a rudder, though once outside someone with enough skill might have managed to sail her home. We could not face each other. Neither of us could bear to see the look of despair in the other's eyes. Our families were foremost in both of our minds, of course, and we were sickened too at having been betrayed by the man we had thought was our friend.

'Let's go up and talk to him,' I said at last. 'He might give it up if we tell him our parents will think we're both dead.'

Brendan made no answer, but he followed me back by the way that we had come. The house door stood open when we reached it. Inside, we found Mr Webb building a turf fire on the hearth. As we came in he struck a match and lit the soft pieces of turf that he was using for kindling. The fire blazed up at once and he stood up and turned to face us. As he did so, the storm struck the house with full force. The door slammed back against the wall, whirling the turf-smoke around the kitchen, and the windows darkened as if someone had suddenly pulled across a heavy curtain. Then we heard a clap of thunder.

'You see,' he said, going over quickly to force the door shut. 'You can't go at all.'

'Is that what you meant?' I asked innocently. 'Did you

know the storm was coming so soon? I would have given it another hour or so –'

'The rudder!' Brendan interrupted me. 'Where is the rudder? You took it out to stop us from going.'

'Sit down and we'll discuss it quietly,' he said, pointing to the chairs which we had ranged around the kitchen table.

'No,' Brendan said. 'I want to know what's happened. Why did you prevent us from going home? Don't you know our families will be frantic with worry – my father and mother – and Dara's – and the little sisters – why did you do it?'

'They'll get over it,' he said easily. 'I noticed that they were letting you go off to Galway without a murmur out of them.'

'We would come back,' I said. 'We were only going to school.'

'And after that?' As we made no answer he went on: 'You know very well that hardly anyone comes back, once they've been away to school.'

'Is that your reason for keeping us here? But why did you teach us, so that we got those scholarships?'

'The pursuit of knowledge needs no reason.'

Suddenly Brendan, the fighter, the one who always had more ideas and courage than anyone else, sat down at the kitchen table and laid his head on his folded arms in an attitude of complete despair. It was that more than anything else that made me realize how utterly we were trapped.

Chapter Six

THERE IS A SAYING IN INISHGLASS, and in other parts of
Ireland too, that when your hand is in the dog's mouth
you should withdraw it very gently. Once I realized that
we had no hope of escape that first day, it seemed more
sensible to appear to go along with Mr Webb's plan.

'I see,' I said after a moment. 'But can't you send our
parents some kind of message?'

'In this weather? You know very well that it's not possible. And if I could do it, they might guess where you
are, which wouldn't suit me at all. Later, perhaps.'

He spoke very quietly and reasonably. No one listening to him would have been able to spot the crazy way his
mind was working. He seemed pained and sad as he
looked down at Brendan's bent head, then he put out
one hand and stroked his shoulder.

'Don't take it so hard,' he said. 'We'll have a good life
together. You both love the islands. You don't want to go
away to live with strangers. As far as your education goes,

I'll teach you everything you need to know.'

Brendan lifted his head and looked at him, but avoided my eye as he said:

'Very well. We'll give it a try.'

So he had the same plan as I had, of appearing to agree.

We would have to wait until we were alone to discuss our next moves. Judging by the howling of the storm around the house, there would be time enough for talk. Even if the rudder had been in the boat when we were at the cove, it would have been risky to try to get away from the island. Now it was ten times worse. Our foolishness in coming in the first place amazed me now, though we couldn't possibly have foreseen this twist in our fate. For the moment, at least, we were safe, in a sound house, with plenty of food and in no danger to our lives.

From then on, Mr Webb assumed we were resigned to staying. He was our master, and though he gave his orders kindly enough it was clear that he expected us to jump to obey him. That first evening he put me in charge of bringing in the turf.

'You can take the creel,' he said, nodding towards the square-shaped willow basket that stood beside the fireplace.

This is what we always use to carry turf on the islands. The comfortable, familiar smell of the turf and the feel of the creel between my hands almost made me weep with longing for home.

Going outside, I had to cling to the door with all my might while I closed it, so that it would not slam back as it had done before. On the doorstep I stood and looked downhill towards the sea. The sky was the colour of ink, the clouds moving and turning and whirling in a mad dance. Across the whole desert of water, westward towards America, the waves were mountains high, heaving and tossing, their curling tops as white as snow as they raced towards the shore. Above my head, seagulls were battling against the wind, uttering their wild, sharp cry.

I turned my eyes away from the horrible sight and went around to the side of the house where the turf-clamp was. I filled the creel frantically, throwing in the sods in bundles, suddenly terrified of the darkening sky and filled with some strange foreboding, as if I were on the edge of an unknown disaster.

With the creel filled, I was hoisting it on to my back by its short rope when I felt a chill like death brush past me. For a long moment I saw the figure of a woman wearing a black skirt to her feet and a checked shawl, as the older women still wear on our islands. Her hair was red-brown, done in the old-fashioned way, and she had large grey eyes. She looked at me steadily, then slowly faded against the dark background of the turf-clamp. At the same moment I heard the unmistakable sound of a crying child.

My feet refused to carry me. I stood perfectly still, the creel on my back, my heart filled with sorrow and pity such as I have never felt before or since. I was not frightened now, as if I knew that the poor spirit of the woman would not wish to injure me. After a minute or so I forced myself to move, walking like someone half-dead the few steps back to the house.

Inside, I kept my head down until I had steadied myself, and placed the creel beside the hearth. When I looked up I saw that the scene was peaceful and home-like. The kettle had already begun to sing over the fire. A little pot with boiling eggs stood on some red cinders from the fire. Brendan was unwrapping plates and mugs from one of the cardboard boxes and laying them on the table, while Mr Webb cut slices from a huge loaf of soda-bread. There was a pat of butter and a pot of jam, and even a plate of his special fruit-cake. Both of them were so busy that they had no time to look at me.

Suddenly I was ravenously hungry. Mr Webb ordered me to make a pot of tea and we had a hearty meal. He kept pressing us to have more bread and butter, saying that one always needs to eat more when the atmospheric pressure is low. Then he gave us a discourse on the causes of storms and the reasons why they are prevalent in some parts of the world and not in others.

'Did Mr Lennon tell you these things in your geography lessons?' he asked with a mischievous look.

'Some of them,' Brendan said. 'Not as much as you've done.'

Mr Webb looked pleased.

'We can always expect storms here,' he said comfortably, 'especially at the time of the equinox. We just have to provide for them. I took along plenty of bread, as you see, and we have about enough for tomorrow. After that we'll have to make our own. Do either of you know how to make bread?'

'My mother makes it always,' I said. 'I never saw my father do it.'

'I'll teach you,' he said. 'Most of the bakers of the world are men.'

Brendan and I dared not look at each other. Everything he said, and especially his tone of voice, made it clear that he was assuming a very long stay for all of us. But surely he would have to renew some of his supplies from time to time. Flour and meal would run out, as well as bread-soda and tea and sugar and soap. These were the things that our parents bought so carefully in the only shop on Inishglass. And he would have to collect his pension money to pay for these things, and for the machinery and equipment he was going to need to build his generator and his reservoir. Obviously he had thought of all this himself. He was too clever to have neglected any detail of his plan.

For the moment, the storm was the best jailer he could possibly have had. From time to time it seemed that gusts shook the house to its foundations. The wind roared in the chimney and sent sparks flying upward from the big fire. As he piled on more turf I began to wonder what I would do if he told me to go outside and get some more. I had no wish to meet the wandering woman again. My only comfort was that ghosts usually come to look once at the new occupants of their territory. This was what I had always heard. Afterwards they don't need to come again.

But she had not yet seen Brendan. If this was her house, as it undoubtedly was, she might well want to come in and have a look at him too, especially as he was a relative of hers. Warning him would do no good. I wondered if she had allowed herself to be seen by Mr Webb.

'Have you ever seen the ghosts here, Mr Webb?'

I asked suddenly. 'You've been here long enough, all alone.'

He gave me a queer, sideways look and said:

'Surely you don't believe in ghosts.'

'Not until I see one,' I said. 'But I've always heard this place called the Island of Ghosts.'

I couldn't go any further without telling him of my experience by the turf-clamp.

'I don't want to disturb any traditions,' he said after a moment. 'If there are ghosts here, they can have no objection to us. They might even be glad to have company again.'

'That's unchristian talk,' Brendan burst out angrily 'Ghosts are uneasy spirits that ought to lie quietly where they were buried, until the Day of Judgement.'

'There are no ghosts,' Mr Webb said firmly. 'Certain tricks of the light can make people imagine thing, especially at dusk or in a half-lit room. Those are only superstitions. What does the priest say?'

'He says we should pray for the dead so that they'll lie easy.'

'No harm in doing that. Does he say that ghosts really walk?'

'He doesn't talk of such things. We're not supposed to have anything to do with the next world.'

'Quite right. We're busy enough in this one.'

I was glad when the conversation dropped. After a while he lit a tall oil-lamp, which he pumped full of air until it gave off a strong white light. He set us to clear away the things from the table and wash them up in the sink by the back door, while he went on with unpacking the boxes. We were dropping with weariness by the time he lit a candle for us and said:

'Time to sleep. Just forget the storm. There's nothing to be afraid of.'

He showed us the room off the kitchen, behind the fireplace, where we were to sleep. There were two new iron beds, and he gave us blankets and sheets for them and told us to make them up. While we were at this Brendan said in a low voice:

'We're going to be a pair of servant boys for him, if he has his way.'

'We'll have to have patience,' I said.

Only the thickness of the wall separated us from the turf-clamp. Since we had come into the room I had been trying to control my terror so as not to frighten Brendan. It was no use. He took my arm and shook it, saying:

'What's the matter? Your face is as white as a sheet. You look as if you had seen a ghost.'

Still I didn't tell him. I asked instead:

'What was the end of the story of those people long ago? What happened to them?'

'Nothing. When the boats came over at the end of the winter they were all dead, the children too. Why are you talking about it? It's a horrible story.'

'I can't get it out of my head. Did they take the bodies back for burial?'

'I don't know. I never heard what they did. I think they couldn't find them all. We'll just have to try to forget it, if we are going to stay here for a while. I wish you wouldn't talk about it.'

He was right, of course. There was certainly no point frightening him too, and now that she had seen me, perhaps the woman would not come again.

We got into bed quickly and were soon asleep, but not for long. All night the wind thundered around the house, several times giving a whistle so sharp that it woke us up. There were no curtains on the windows, and the darkness was streaked with light from a full moon, which seemed to dart in and out through the galloping clouds. I buried my head under the pillow in fear of what I would see, and fell asleep again.

The morning brought no lessening of the storm. The white light at the window awakened us. We could hear Mr Webb moving about in the kitchen, filling the kettle, stirring up the fire, then laying on fresh turf. We dressed quickly and went into the kitchen. This would have been our last day at home, before going to the school in Galway, but neither of us spoke of that.

As the morning went on I found that the night's sleep had brought me resignation, or perhaps despair. Whatever it was, it made our situation easier to bear. I no longer felt the need to fight every inch of the way. We were here, prisoners, in the hands of Mr Webb, and we must bow our heads and accept it. I hoped that Brendan felt the same, but there was no point in asking him.

Soon it was clear that Mr Webb had carefully thought out how we were to occupy our time. Immediately after breakfast he set me to make a loaf of bread. I had often watched my mother do it, with flour and salt and bread-soda buttermilk, kneading it expertly on the kitchen table until she had a big round loaf which she baked on the hearth in the pot-oven. I soon found that it was quite another thing to do it myself. First I used too much milk, so that the pieces of dough got hopelessly tangled in my fingers. When I put in more flour, the mixture became so dry that I had to leave it to Mr Webb to finish. He splashed in some more milk and gathered the dough together, and in no time he had a perfectly shaped loaf.

'You'll learn soon enough,' he said. 'There's no hurry.

In a few months you'll be a master baker.'

I thought it better to make no answer to that.

In the meantime Brendan was cleaning out the hen-house and collecting the eggs. Since early morning we had heard the hens boasting as each one was laid. There were eight of them, and Mr Webb looked as proud of them as if he had laid them himself.

When the bread was baked we went out to see to the goats. They were waiting for us, crowded into a corner of the field, sheltering from the storm and glad to part with their milk.

'Goats are less complicated than cows,' Mr Webb said. 'We'd have to keep a bull, and this island is too small for that. Goats are healthy creatures, and since they never get tuberculosis, there is no need to boil the milk.'

'What about butter?' I asked.

'We'll have to buy that ashore,' he said. 'I have plenty in stock at present, enough for the rest of the winter. We won't go short. We can make cheese of the goats' milk and of the sheep's milk too. Next year we can separate some of the sheep and keep them in a pen, and milk them every day just like the goats. We should have quite a big herd of goats in the spring, if these have one kid each.'

The idea of milking a sheep was strange to us. Usually

the lambs took care of that. But what made our hearts sink as heavy as lead was the casual way he talked of the supply of butter for the rest of the winter, and his plans for next spring, as if he had not the smallest doubt that we would be there to share his life forever.

After we had brought the milk home, he set us to unpack his books and put them on the shelves he had brought from Inishglass.

'These will be your university,' he said. 'Once you have read them all, you'll have no further need of school.'

There were many volumes of an encyclopaedia, and presently he set us at the kitchen table with a volume each. I was to read the article on Greece and Brendan the one on the Latin language and its literature. When we had finished, he gave us our first lessons in Latin and Greek. We paused for a while to cook and eat dinner, and then we had lessons in geography and mathematics.

The light was beginning to fade when he said at last:

'Time for some exercise. Fresh air and exercise are as important as food and sleep.'

Chapter Seven

WE COULDN'T HAVE HAD A GAME OF FOOTBALL in that storm, even if he had brought a ball along. A walk around the island would have been welcome, but there was to be nothing as frivolous as that. Instead Brendan was sent to the well for water, and I had to bring in a creel of turf. Then Mr Webb said:

'Now we can work for a couple of hours on the waterfall before it gets too dark. That will be our source of electricity when we get the turbine going. There is a higher well that we'll use for the reservoir.'

We took the shovels he gave us and went out to the stream, where he set us to work. There was no chance of private conversation. He stayed so close to us that he would have heard every word.

The stream that flowed out of the well was strong and clear. Some time before, Mr Webb had widened its banks and constructed a tiny weir of flat stones, over which the water fell smoothly. Our work was to deepen this fall, standing with bare feet in the water, digging with our shovels, then lifting out the stones and throwing them up on the bank. It was back-breaking work, and to make things worse the storm was still raging around us, blowing our wet clothes against us and threatening to knock us over into the water. The only comfort was the knowledge that it would eventually get dark.

'The wind doesn't matter,' Mr Webb said cheerfully. 'I know you don't mind getting wet. If we can get this done before the weather gets really cold, we'll be off to a good start in the spring.'

His job was to shovel away the stones that we lifted out of the bed of the stream and build them into a little wall at one side. He piled the gravel between this wall and the stream.

'Later we can cement it into position,' he said. 'When we get heavy rain, the stream will clean itself out. Always let nature do as much work for you as possible.'

As time went on I noticed that Brendan was getting more and more impatient. Not even the men work like this on Inishglass, nor indeed on any of the islands, as you will notice at once if you ever visit there. For boys it was a completely new idea. We had always been told that it was our business to enjoy life and grow up healthy. Though we did some part in the farm work, our contribution was never taken seriously. We had both heard of the bad old times when boys and young men were hired by mean mainland farmers, who made them get up early and slave all day for small wages and smaller rations. There were several songs about them – 'The Rocks of Bawn' and 'The Galbally Farmer' were two that I had often heard. Such behaviour had gone out in our grandfathers' time. Apart from our main grievance of having been kidnapped, we were both outraged at this treatment, Brendan far more than I was, as it turned out.

His chance came when the handle of Mr Webb's shovel broke.

'Carry on!' he called out to us. 'I'll just go and get another.'

And he swung off to the house as if he had plenty of energy left. When he was ten yards away Brendan said:

'When he comes back, we'll jump on him together.'

'What do you mean? Knock him down?'

'Of course. What else can we do? Are you willing to spend the rest of your life locked up with this lunatic, taking his orders, working like a horse?'

'No. But do you think we can do it?'

'Of course we can. There are two of us. He's only one. Where's your guts?'

'What use would it be?'

'We can keep him tied up and force him to tell us where the rudder of the boat is, or make ourselves another one out of some of his bits of wood. I hope the boat is still there, after this storm. You heard him saying, "Always let nature do as much work for you as possible." That means us, and he's going to work us to death if we don't stop him. Did you notice that he never got his own feet wet? He has two slaves now, and that's what we'll be forever if we don't make a run for it.'

I knew that he was right, and still I was sad at the idea of attacking one whose company I had so much enjoyed, and who had done so much for us.

There was no time to spare for working it out. Here he came marching back to us, with a new shovel carried over his shoulder like a gun.

The stream was shallow where we were standing, no more than two feet deep. We waited until he was at work again, then with one leap we were out of the stream and on his back.

After that everything happened in a flash. One moment we were on top, holding him down. A moment later he had given a kind of flick with his body and thrown us off, sending me flying a yard off. As I sprang to my feet, I saw him hurl Brendan away, so that he landed on his back in the stream with the water flowing over him.

'He'll drown!' I shouted at the top of my voice.

Mr Webb was standing up, dusting the sleeve of his jacket with his hands.

'He certainly will, if you don't get him out,' he said in a rasping tone. 'Get down there and lift his head.'

I jumped into the stream and did as he said, and then he helped me to haul Brendan on to the bank, where he lay spitting out water, moaning pitifully.

'I'm sorry about this,' Mr Webb said. 'I should have warned you not to try anything. I learned a few tricks like that in my travels around the world. Now I'm afraid poor Brendan has injured himself.'

When we tried to stand him up, his face turned white and he fainted dead away. A line of bright-red blood flowed over his right ankle.

'I thought so,' Mr Webb said with satisfaction. 'He has broken his leg. A tourniquet first, and then we'll make a cat's cradle and carry him home.'

He cut off the leg of Brendan's trousers with one long slice of a wicked-looking knife that he carried in his pocket, exposing the ugly, twisted limb. He made me keep my thumb on the artery to the back of Brendan's knee while he tied the leg tightly with his big handkerchief, placing the knot over the artery to stop the bleeding. Then he showed me how to make the cat's cradle, with our arms intertwined in a kind of basket arrangement. We got under Brendan's inert body and lifted him up. Very carefully, at a snail's pace, we carried him back to the house and laid him on his bed. The broken leg was twisted unnaturally sideways, and blood had begun to seep through the tourniquet and on to the blanket. Mr Webb stood looking down at him.

'His idea, I think,' he said after a moment. 'Well, there's some justice in what has happened to him. He won't be able to move for a long time. It's just as well that there are two of us here to look after him.'

That was when I saw the woman again. Darkness had almost fallen and the room was in twilight, lit only by one small window. She stood for a minute beside the bed, gazing down at Brendan, her face full of pain and sorrow. Then she looked directly at me and a moment later she faded away into the dimness of the far corner.

Mr Webb seemed to have seen nothing, nor to have noticed my agitation. When I had recovered enough to look at him he was saying briskly:

'Now is the time to begin your medical education.'

I soon saw that it was another of his special skills, wherever he had picked it up.

'Boiling water, in a basin,' he said, without turning his head. 'Bring the first-aid box too. I didn't think we would need it so soon.'

I was glad to get out of the room. The sight of the broken shin-bone sticking out through the skin was enough to make me queasy, and Brendan's face was so white and still. Above all, the visit from the tormented spirit of the woman had left me with a feeling of complete despair for our future. I could not rid myself of the idea that she was inviting us to come and join her, in the dim next world where she was held captive. I knew these thoughts were not right nor Christian but they were embedded in my brain all the same.

The kettle was singing above the fire and I splashed some water into the washing-up basin, reflecting as I did so that if we had had our way the patient would have been Mr Webb. I could see now how foolish we had been, not even a rope handy to tie him up with, nor a plan of any sort for taking him back to the house and keeping him a prisoner. I realized too that we must have thought his age would make him an easy captive.

Try as I would now, I couldn't remember exactly what he had done to throw us off so easily. He had said himself that it was not the first time he had done such a thing. After our attempt to capture him, it seemed likely that we would never hear the full story of his life. The little he had told us had come out so grudgingly that one could see he had no wish to talk about his past, even when we were friends. Had he said something about South America? I couldn't remember.

The first-aid box contained cotton wool and swabs and bandages and several splints, as well as surgical needles and sutures for repairing bad cuts, almost as if Mr Webb had been expecting disaster to strike us. When I got back into the bedroom, he had pressed the bone back into place. Brendan was moaning but he was still unconscious.

'Just as well he fainted again,' Mr Webb said. 'I've never learned to give an anaesthetic except with whiskey.'

He made me hold the basin close. Then he picked up cotton wool with a forceps and dipped it in the boiling water. I watched, fascinated, while he cleaned off the skin carefully, then swabbed it with disinfectant and stitched it as neatly as a woman making an apron. Finally he placed the splint and bandaged it expertly. When he had finished he said:

'I don't know whether or not that is going to heal, or whether he has lamed himself for life. If we could get him to hospital they'd put him in plaster. This will have to do now.'

The cool way he stated that Brendan had lamed himself amazed me. Obviously he felt no responsibility at all for what had happened. You may be sure that I had no wish to argue with him. At least Brendan was safe for the moment. He was still in a dead faint and his face was a greenish white, but his breathing was more regular.

We got the rest of his clothes off and put him into bed, under the blankets, heaving him around like a sack. He moaned while we were moving him but when he was lying still he looked more comfortable.

'The only pain-killer I have is aspirin,' Mr Webb said. 'You can give him four during the night but you'll have to space them out, else he might begin to bleed.'

I looked at him without a word. It would be useless, even ridiculous, to protest at having to nurse Brendan, since I had been in the conspiracy too. We went back to the kitchen, leaving the door open so that we could hear Brendan when he woke up. Then there were the goats to be milked and the hens to shut in for the night, and the tools that we had left on the bank of the stream to be brought home. Everything had to be done at speed, in the half-dark. There was no sign of the storm dying out. If anything it was worse than ever. It would have been a comfort to have gone down to the cove and made sure that the *gleoiteog* was safe, even rudderless as she was, but

I wouldn't have dared to try it.

When I came back with the cans of milk I found Mr Webb had lit the big lamp in the kitchen. He had also lit a small oil-lamp and left it on the chest in our room. I went in at once to look at Brendan. In the soft yellow light he looked less pale and listless. His eyes were still shut and every now and then he moaned with pain. I stayed with him for a moment only, before Mr Webb called out from the kitchen:

'Come along, there. No point in wasting time. We've got to cook a meal.'

We boiled potatoes and some dried fish, which might not please everyone but it was the food I had been used to all my life. It was a great comfort to me, and I found that it had given me back some of my courage. After we had eaten he made me wash up the plates before he allowed me to visit Brendan again. This time his eyes were open and he looked at me without speaking.

'Your leg is broken,' I said softly. 'You fell into the stream.'

'I remember.' He closed his eyes, then said: 'What about you?'

'Nothing. I'm all right. You'll just have to lie here and get well.'

'Will I get well?'

'Yes, of course. Bardal set the bone as if he had been doing it all his life. But he says it will take a long time.' I knew very well what painful thoughts were in his mind but there was nothing I could do to ease them. 'Would you like some milk?'

'Yes.'

Back in the kitchen, I put some milk to warm on a hot coal from the fire. Mr Webb was watching me.

'So he's awake,' he said after a while.

'Yes.'

'Has he asked what happened?'

'He remembers.'

'That's a good sign. Milk will be all right. He can have some bread and butter later.'

I made no answer. He watched me pour the milk into a mug.

'This is a great complication,' he said then. 'You and I will have to do his work as well as our own. A lot of the plans will have to be put off until he's well again. I was working on a method of harnessing the tide to make electricity. That was going to be very interesting. I'll show you the paper-work. Brendan is good at these things too. Now we'll have to wait.'

He spoke so sadly and sounded so sincere that I felt my bitterness towards him lessen. His dream, Hy-

Breasail, filled his mind completely, leaving no room for anything else. It was as if his genius had him in its power, so that he no longer cared about the needs of anyone outside of himself. When I understood this, I felt a pang of pity for him, though I knew it was dangerous to soften in any way.

I took the milk into the bedroom and held Brendan's head up while he drank it. When he lay back on the pillow and seemed to fall asleep, I turned the lamp low and went back into the kitchen. Mr Webb's mood had changed completely. He was sitting at the table with a game-board in front of him.

'Come along,' he said cheerfully. 'Scrabble. This is the best way to improve your knowledge of English. Pull in your chair. I'll show you how to play it.' He looked at me sharply. 'No point in fussing over him, once we've done everything we can. I'll teach you how to nurse him so that he won't suffer any ill effects.'

It was the first sign of a return to our old friendship. I was so grateful for this that I could not bring myself to be surly with him. I did as he said, and we began on the game.

Chapter Eight

THE NEXT PART OF THE STORY BELONGS TO ME, Barbara, Dara's sister, and to Cáit, my best friend. As Dara has said, though he and Brendan were a year older than us, we four were always together since we sat near each other at school. We all sang the little songs together in the infants' part of the school:

Hi-diddle-dum, the cat and his mother
Went off to Galway riding a drake.
Hi-diddle-dum, the rain came down,
They both fell off and were drowned in the lake.

Another song was:

The cow, the cow, the one-horned cow
She's lost on the hill and I'll never find her now.

Then the boys moved into the other part of the school and began to learn serious things, like sums and spelling, but they never thought they were too big for us all to play together.

The day they disappeared, though we knew it was their last one at home, we had to stay at school until three o'clock. As soon as we were free, we ran first to Cáit's house, expecting to find the boys there. Cáit's aunt, Nellie Mór, was sitting in her usual place on the big rock by the front door.

'Gone off to swim, if you please, down to the Horses' Strand,' she said. 'Their last day and they couldn't spend it at home. There's boys for you.'

We were disappointed, naturally, but as we walked up to our house I said:

'I know they wouldn't go off for the whole day. They'd know we would be looking for them after school.'

But now we both remembered that they had told us nothing yesterday about their plans for the morning. My mother said that they hadn't taken much food with them.

'They'll be back very soon,' she said. 'Nothing to give you an appetite like a swim. Why don't you go to meet them?'

Going up the hill past Bardal's house, we noticed that the door was shut. We saw nothing unusual in this. We went past quietly, not wanting to get into conversation with him, thinking that he might open the door suddenly and call us in. We had no time for anyone today but the two boys that were going into exile.

At the top of the hill we stopped and looked down towards the sea. It was perfectly calm, glittering in the sun, with only a single small cloud off to the west to show that there might be a storm coming.

We continued down the hill a little way, until we could see the whole curve of the strand laid out before us. Cáit was the first to get uneasy.

'I don't see them.' she said. 'If they'd forgotten the time, they would be jumping in and out of the water on a day like this.'

'Perhaps they've come up already,' I said.

But we knew they couldn't have, because they would certainly have met us on the way. With only one road you're never in any doubt about where everyone is. Still, we went down to the strand and had a closer look. After a while Cáit said:

'They never came here at all. There are no footmarks, even above the tide-mark. Bran would have left scuffle marks in the sand. No one has been here all day.'

'Then where did they go?'

'We'll go back and ask Bardal. Perhaps they went somewhere with him instead.'

Bardal's door was locked. We knocked, and waited for a few minutes, not knowing what to do. Then I said:

'I'm going to look in through the windows.'

Cáit was shocked.

'That would be very bad manners.'

'I'm past manners,' I said. 'I think something has happened to them.'

I climbed on to the window-sill and peered through the glass, but at first I could see nothing. Little by little I was able to get a view of the room where the boys had spent so many hours, sitting at the kitchen table with Bardal, and where we had come ourselves at last to make friends with him. What I saw nearly made me fall off the windowsill. I climbed down carefully, saying:

'Everything is gone out of the house – the dresser – the table – the chairs – everything.'

Cáit wouldn't believe me until she had climbed up and seen for herself. We went around to the back of the house. There was a shed there, where Bardal kept his tools. It was padlocked but we were able to see through a crack in the door that it was empty too. We felt like crying with disappointment. Here was a big secret, and we had been kept right out of it. Around at the front again, I said:

'If they were going off somewhere with him, they should have told us. This is mean of them.'

'They're never mean,' Cáit said. 'It's something else.'

'Perhaps Bardal asked them to go with him to Carraroe.

He's always running over there lately.'

'But taking his furniture! And they wouldn't have gone so far without telling it at home.'

'Perhaps it's Bardal's secret. Perhaps he asked them not to tell.'

'And Bran – where is he? Dara wouldn't go anywhere without him, I'm sure.'

Still we felt that it was too soon to get frightened.

'But we can't go home yet,' Cáit said. 'My aunt Nellie would have the whole island out looking for them at once. Nothing she likes so much as a bit of excitement and trouble.'

Then I thought of going down to the cove to see if Mr Webb's boat was there. The day had darkened and the north-west wind had begun to blow. From the cliff above the cove we could see that the waves were mounting higher and higher. There was no sign of the *gleoiteog*. We climbed down between the rocks by the gravelly path, and came out at Bardal's moorings.

Suddenly we saw Bran, sitting upright at his look-out post above the cove. In a moment he came leaping down, rushing at us and barking wildly. We hugged him frantic-ally, asking him over and over:

'Where are they? Go and find them – where are they?'

He answered us as best he could by running back and

forth to the edge of the water, barking and jumping up and down impatiently, clearly wanting us to produce a boat by magic and sail out of the cove.

'They've gone with Bardal, all right,' I said. 'If the storm keeps on like this, they won't be able to get back. They'll have to stay in Carraroe or Carna or wherever they land.'

'But they're supposed to go to Galway tomorrow, to school.'

'Then they'll have to go by the bus. We won't see them again until Christmas.'

'Their clothes –'

I couldn't imagine what could be done about that.

'I suppose everything will have to be sent after them.' I said uncertainly. 'Anyway, that's the least important thing.'

We knew we would have to tell our families what we had discovered, especially now that we had found Bran. Still we waited a little longer, hoping perhaps that we would see the *gleoiteog* come sailing into the cove before the storm. A storm it was beginning to be, by this time, the waves racing up between the rocks so that we had to skip out of the way before them. Bran had gone back to gaze out to sea, but we called him down to us. He came reluctantly, crouching on the ground and sidling along as he always did when he didn't want to obey. He followed us up the gully and back to Mr Webb's house. There he stopped, and we had to call him over and over again before he agreed to follow us the rest of the way home.

We went first to our house. My mother was sweeping the doorstep. I can still see her, stopping suddenly, holding the brush as if she were clinging to it for support. She called out at once:

'What's happened? Where are they? Why aren't they with you? The dog –'

She had guessed by our looks that it was some disaster. We made no answer, knowing that neighbours were coming to their doors to hear what was happening. She waited until we were inside the house before asking any more.

'We know nothing,' I said. 'Bran was below at the cove, looking out as if he saw them go that way. Bardal's boat is gone.'

'Did they say anything to you about where they were going?'

'Not a word.'

'Did they say they'd see you after school?'

'They didn't say they wouldn't.'

'We didn't notice at the time but now I remember that they made no plan at all,' Cáit said.

My father came in from his little office asking anxiously:

'What's happened? Where are the boys?'

Then we had to tell our story again, and after that it was no more of our business. By this time the storm had taken over the whole island. From our door we could see the men running to their boats and the women gathering in the hens and ducks and the small animals, and putting them into their sheds for safety.

'It's a regular hurricane, according to the wireless,' my father said. He looked at my mother. 'They'll be safe somewhere, if they left in the morning.'

'We don't know what time they left.'

My father went back into his office to telephone to the post offices in Carraroe and Carna. He came back into the kitchen very quietly and sat down at the table with his head down. My mother shook his shoulder, asking in a whisper:

'Well? What did you hear?'

'A *gleoiteog* lost – a mile offshore. Everyone in Mweenish was out watching it. The storm was pounding it. It keeled over, capsized, the sails beating the water – like a dying fish, he said.'

'Who? When?'

'A few minutes ago, maybe half an hour. A man that

was in the post office with Máirtín Costello in Carna told me he saw it. He said everyone thought it must be from the islands. All of their boats are in.'

As long as I live I'll never forget that day. My parents went running down to Brendan's house with the terrible news and soon the whole island was mourning. A procession of old and young came offering sympathy. My mother's sister Kate came from her own house and made pots and pots of tea for the visitors. The same was going on in Cáit's house. Down there, some of the old women had started keening. The wild, strange sound was carried to us on the wind. My mother wouldn't have allowed that in our house, but Nellie Mór had started it and she would not let it be stopped.

No one took any notice of us. Cáit and I sat huddled together on the bench by the fire, with Bran at our feet, not daring to speak in case we would have to tell our story again. I felt that if I had to say their names, I would die of sorrow. I could barely look at my mother's face. In that one afternoon she had suddenly changed into an old, old woman. Above all my father's grief broke my heart. He didn't weep, just sat at the table looking bewildered, as if he simply could not understand what had happened.

Still the storm thundered on, sometimes shaking the house with a heavy gust so that it seemed it would level it to the ground. Every voice was lowered to a whisper, as if the people didn't want the wind to hear them.

'Sure, they're gone straight to heaven,' the old women said. 'Two innocent boys. Isn't it grand for them?'

No one contradicted that but the young women looked at each other in desperation. The men sat silently, close to my father, smoking their pipes and saying nothing at all.

All through the night they stayed, while Cáit and I slept off and on in each other's arms. In the cold dawn someone made us go to bed and we lay until far into the day in my parents' big bed, dozing now and then and waking to hear the soft voices still murmuring in the kitchen.

In the afternoon I lay on my back and stretched out my hand to see if Cáit was awake. She took hold of my hand and we lay there quietly for a few minutes.

'I can't help thinking we'll see them again,' I said then.

'In heaven, the way the old women said?'

'No, here on earth. I think they're still alive.'

'But the *gleoiteog* that was lost – everyone saw it.'

'They didn't see who was in it. I don't believe that was Bardal's boat.'

'Why not? Whose boat could it be?'

'Someone else's. Can you imagine Bardal being stupid enough to get caught in a storm like this?'

'No. That thought has been in my mind all night. He knows too much.'

We were quiet for a while then, listening to the storm. No one in this world could be clever enough to live through it. Lying in the bed we could see through the little window how the huge grey and white waves stretched taller and taller, then came cascading down in a great avalanche, all white with foam, racing towards the shore. One could scarcely believe that this was the same shore where we had played with the soft white sand so recently.

'There's only one place where they could be,' Cáit said at last.

'I know. On the Island of Ghosts. Bardal was always talking about it. He said he goes there often.'

'Then we must tell everyone at once.'

'They won't believe us. They'll say we're rambling in our minds.'

After a while we got up and joined the company in the kitchen. All evening, we watched and waited for a chance to tell what we were thinking. Once I went and sat quietly beside my Aunt Kate, saying softly:

'No one is sure that they were on that boat. The wreck

hasn't been found. Couldn't they have landed on the Island of Ghosts, or some other island, or farther up the coast?'

'God help you, child, there's no hope of that,' she said. 'While you were asleep, your father has telephoned to every single place where they might be missing a boat, and they're all safe and sound.'

At this all my hopes were quenched like a candle and I was left in the darkness of despair.

Chapter Nine

THE STORM DIED DOWN after a few days and the other children who had won scholarships went off to Galway to their boarding-schools. Cáit and I tried to carry on as if nothing had happened to us, but at school neither of us could do anything right and Mr Lennon was beginning to lose patience. He came stumping up to our house one afternoon and glared at me angrily, then said to my father:

'They're like two little widows. When I ask them a question, they look at me as if they didn't even hear me. Their heads are in the clouds. They've forgotten everything they ever knew. They should be working for scholarships like their brothers but at the rate they're going they'll never be fit.'

My father heard him out, then said sadly:

'Give them time. They're like little widows, indeed, God help us all. Give them time. It cures everything, in the end.'

Though nobody liked poor Mr Lennon, my mother

made him sit down in the kitchen and drink some tea. She signalled to me to leave her alone with him, and then she sat beside him and made him talk as he had never done before. It was she who found out that he was plunged as deep in grief as anyone else on the island, after the two lost boys. She never told exactly what they said to each other, but I saw that when he went home at last, he kissed her hand and said:

'God bless you for a great-hearted lady. Tonight I'll sleep easy for the first time.'

Maggie Cooney had dropped in at that moment to borrow a cup of sugar or to find out why Mr Lennon was staying so long. Now she let out a shriek of laughter and said half to herself:

'*Musha*, lady!'

My mother gave her such a furious look that ever after she went to borrow what she needed from her neighbour at the other side of the road, a relief to us all.

So we were allowed to skip school sometimes and go off for walks together, when the pain became too much for us. Bran always came with us, delighted at first to be taken for an outing. Then as he remembered his misery he would begin to slide along the ground, turning to look at us now and then as if to make sure that we hadn't deserted him too.

We often went past Bardal's house but we kept our eyes down, and we never again went to look through the windows. Like everyone else on Inishglass, secretly we blamed Bardal for the loss of the boys. No one had said it, and the prayers for the dead always included his name, but we all felt that as a stranger he had broken the rules of hospitality in taking them out in his boat without their parents' knowledge.

As the darker winter evenings began, it was harder for us to be alone, and we had to be very careful not to be overheard. Everyone would have thought that our conversation was unhealthy, even unchristian, since it showed that we didn't accept the will of God. From the beginning of time, island people have had to come to terms with what the sea can do to them, and to realise that they can't fight it. We were going against every piece of wisdom that our ancestors had learned through the centuries: unless we had seen that boat sink, we couldn't believe that Mr Webb and the boys were drowned. I won't try to make sense of this. There was no sense in it. But we were as certain as if we had proof from heaven.

Whatever people would have thought of our idea that the boys were alive, they would surely have said we were touched in the head if they knew that we believed they were on the Island of Ghosts. The more we talked about it, the more sure we were that this was where we would find them. We went over and over the conversation with Mr Webb, when he had talked so longingly about the island. We remembered that he had asked the boys if they would be afraid to go there, and had said that it would be a good place to live. He had been there several times, and he compared it with Hy-Breasail. He had talked about the beautiful grassland – sixty acres of it – and said he didn't believe it was haunted by ghosts. We were not quite sure about that last part but he had certainly not believed the ghosts were a reason for leaving the island barren and uninhabited.

Supposing he had taken the boys there for a trip in the *gleoiteog* and that they had been cast away, and the boat lost, swept off to sea in that awful storm? As time went on we became convinced that this must have been what happened.

'But we'll never get anyone to believe us,' Cáit said sadly. 'The men would as soon set sail for America as they would for the Island of Ghosts, especially if they were sent to look for people that they think are dead.'

'Surely there is someone who would listen to us,' I said.

It seemed so reasonable, and still we couldn't think of anyone on the island who would take our idea seriously enough to act on it. In both of our houses, the sad faces of our parents made it impossible to speak of the boys at all.

We could see how they were trying their best to keep on living as they always did, each day hoping their pain would get less. This was as much for our sake as for their own. It would have seemed heartless and cruel to have lighted up even a small flash of hope, on nothing more than instinct and intuition.

'And still we can't just leave them there,' I said one day, when we were talking over the whole thing as usual, lying on my bed with Bran between us, and keeping our voices low. 'If we were boys, we could take a boat and go and have a look for ourselves.'

'Girls and boys don't come into it. Girls are pilots on aircraft now,' Cáit said. 'There are three or four of them in Irish Airlines, flying to Rome and New York – all over the world. I read that in the paper that came with the post, only a few days ago.'

'All the same, it will be a long time before we'll be allowed out in a boat.'

'Then we'll have to go without leave,' Cáit said. 'I suppose we always knew that.'

'How? When?'

'We know how to sail a boat, from watching the men.'

'It's harder than it looks. And we haven't got a boat to sail.'

'No one would take us.'

'We can't keep going over and over it,' I said. 'We'll have to think it all out and make a good plan. That's the only way.'

'Begin with the boat, then,' Cáit said after a moment. 'We can do nothing without one.'

'Who would lend us a boat?'

'Or where could we steal one?'

I didn't like that idea. A boat was a family's living, even if we could manage to steal one, which I thought very unlikely.

'You know we'd never get away with it,' I said. 'The only way is to get one honestly.'

'In Carraroe?'

'The story would be here before us, if we tried that.'

'In Galway, then.'

'We'd have to sail out along the Bay. Whatever about getting over to the Island of Ghosts from here, we'd have no hope of sailing from Galway. There must be some way of doing it. Think – think hard.'

We thought until our heads hurt. Unless we could get one of our neighbours to help us, we had no hope whatever.

'If we can't get help, we can't do it at all,' I said.

'Who?'

'Someone that's a bit crazy, like ourselves.'

'My Aunt Nellie?'

'She's crazy enough for anything but she'd tell it to the birds – she'd have the story in America before we could move a toe.'

'We could tell her to keep it a secret.'

'She doesn't know what that word means. She'd start by letting out hints and in a day or two she'd have it all over the island. Forget about her,' I said impatiently. 'Oddity is only one qualification. There must be someone else. The person we need must have some wits.'

'And a boat.'

'Mr Lennon.'

We lay silently for a long time, thinking about him. It was true that he was the perfect person to help us. He was the most silent man on the whole of Inishglass. If he met one of his neighbours on the road between his house and the school, all he would give was a sort of grunt, while the other man would call out a blessing and an opinion on the weather. No one expected anything better of him, at this stage. Until the day he talked to my mother, I had never seen him in friendly conversation with anyone except the children in the school. Even with us he was often surly enough, but we didn't care because we knew he was surly with everyone, and we knew he cared a great deal about our welfare. When he went to the shop or to Flaherty's pub for a pint of beer, he never had anything to say except perhaps some complaint against the Government, addressed to no one in particular. All the men had long ago given him up, though they were always very polite to him because of his learning and his important position.

And he had a boat. It was a *gleoiteog*, like Mr Webb's but smaller. He bought it soon after he came to the island, from Matthew Daly's widow. He kept it as carefully as an old woman's cat in the little cove below his house, tending it and caulking it and tarring it year by year, hardly ever taking it on the water. Three or four times each summer he would launch it himself, refusing all help, choosing a day when the wind and the tides were perfect. He never went more than a few miles, always out to sea, always quite alone. My father said that in the beginning some of the men had offered to go with him, to help him with some fishing, but he had declined their offers roughly, saying that he never fished. Seeing the lovely boat lying idle, once Cumeen Peter asked if he could borrow it.

'Yes,' said Mr Lennon, 'if you will lend me your wife.'

That was the last time anyone thought of asking for that boat. We had often heard the men talking about it, sniggering among themselves at Mr Lennon's joke, but they hadn't liked him any the better for it.

'I wonder what he would say to us, if we asked him,' Cáit said. 'He knows us, and he knows how we're suffering. I don't believe he would be nasty about it.'

'There's only one way to find out,' I said, 'and that's to go and ask him. What does it matter if he's nasty? When the worst thing has happened, you don't care much about the little things.'

Cáit agreed, and still we were terrified at the thought of going to his house and telling him of our plan. But we had picked him out as the only person on the whole island who might listen to us. If we were afraid to ask him, it meant that we would do nothing at all, now or ever, to search for our two friends.

'Next Saturday, then,' I said.

We didn't speak of our plan in the days between. Perhaps each of us was afraid that the other would have lost heart and changed her mind. When Saturday came, we were in a panic. If you knew Mr Lennon as we did, you would understand that better. He was like a bull, or a circus lion – you never knew how the humour would take him.

Luckily it was a fine sunny day, though those are rare in early December. The sea was like glass and there was scarcely a cloud in the sky. The boreen that led to Mr Lennon's house was bordered by a busy little stream which was now in full flood, rattling loudly over the stones, sometimes making a dark waterfall and broadening out into a pool. The sun glittered and sparkled on the water, and warmed our backs as we walked along. Bran trotted behind us, every move showing his pleasure. We had no need to talk. We had made no plan, since we didn't know what to expect, nor even whether we would be allowed to speak at all.

Mr Lennon was sitting at his kitchen table, with a pile of exercise books in front of him. He looked up sharply, with the furious expression that we knew so well, and which meant he had been reading some piece of stupidity written by one of his pupils. One glance told me that the page in front of him had not been written by either of us. For one thing, it had a big ink-blot on one corner, and we knew better than to let that happen.

Then his face cleared and he gave us quite a kindly look and said:

'Come in, come in. Sit down.'

The two other chairs were covered with books, which he had to throw on the floor before he could pull them forward for us. It was easy to see that he had had no visitors for a while. We sat awkwardly, clutching our hands together, not knowing how to begin, while he watched us with the same friendly eyes. I had never before noticed what a bright brown they were, with changing lights like the pool below the waterfall in the stream outside. Perhaps it was this that left us tongue-tied until he said:

'I'm glad you came to see me. You have something to say. I can tell by the way you looked at each other as you came in.'

'It's about the boys,' I said, speaking much too loud because of my nervousness. Then, in a voice scarcely above a whisper I went on: 'We don't believe they're drowned at all.'

We were both afraid to look at him now. As soon as I had said it, I realized that we must seem a pair of little fools. Cáit clearly felt the same. She was studying her jumping hands as if she had never seen them do things like this before. I leaned down to pull Bran's ears, where he lay crouched under my chair. I wished we were a mile away, and that we had never thought of this crazy plan. I couldn't imagine how we would ever look Mr Lennon in the face again.

Then, to my amazement, I heard him say:

'I've never believed it.'

'Why?'

'Why not?'

Now we had both forgotten our fears and were watching him eagerly. I could see he was amused by the change in us.

'Mr Webb is a clever man,' he said slowly. 'I thought he wouldn't be likely to do anything foolish.'

'But his wife was killed in a plane crash in California. They took risks.'

'He told you that, did he?'

'No. He told the boys. They told us. Is it true?'

'Of course it's true. He doesn't talk about himself, but I was curious about him. I found an account of him in an old magazine in the library in Galway, all about his wife too, and the research they had done, and how she died. I wondered why he was living here when he didn't have to. I think he came to Inishglass to escape from the world, but I could have told him it's not so easy to do that. He would take a risk to do something that he thought important, but he would never take one just from idleness, or because he wanted an outing on a fine day.' All at once he gave us his familiar glare, so that we almost fell off our chairs, then snapped out: 'What's your idea?'

'We think he took the boys to the Island of Ghosts. He was always talking about it. We think they're there, safe and sound, but no one on Inishglass would go out there and find them.'

'Would you?'

'We would do anything to get them back, or even to find out that they're really gone for good. Until we're sure, one way or another, we might as well be dead ourselves.'

There was a long pause, which we couldn't break. He was back to the state we knew, eyes narrowed, mouth twisted on one side. I wondered how we had ever managed to speak to him. Suddenly he said, with a kind of bark:

'What do you want from me?'

From the depths of my despair I said:

'Your boat, so that we can sail to the Island of Ghosts and see for ourselves.'

He covered the lower half of his face with one hand and stared at us out of those bright brown eyes. We had not the faintest idea what was in his mind. I stood up to go, saying:

'We're wasting your time. I'm sorry.'

'Sit down, girl,' he said. 'Of course I'll help you. Now we must put our heads together and work out what we're going to do.'

Chapter Ten

THE IDEA OF PUTTING OUR HEADS TOGETHER with Mr Lennon made me laugh, and I saw that Cáit had seen the joke of it too. Bran came out from under my chair and waggled his body at each of us in turn, sensing friendship in the air. Then he went to sit by the little smoky fire, his nose in his paws and his eyes rolling as he kept a close watch on us.

Mr Lennon asked the most important question at once:

'Do either of you know how to sail a boat?'

'We haven't been allowed out in a *púcán* nor in a *gleoiteog* for years,' I said. 'The last time I went out in our *púcán* was on my tenth birthday. I screamed and yelled so hard that my mother let me go with my father in the end, but she said she would never agree to it again. Girls aren't supposed to go in the boats.'

'Did you ask any of the boys to help you?'

'No. We didn't trust them not to tell what was in our

minds. Besides, they wouldn't be let out in a boat now either, after what has happened.'

'True. And you're too big to scream and yell. How much do you remember about sailing?'

'Everything I saw the men do. My father let me hold a rope but I found it very heavy when my hands were so small.'

'It's still heavy. Do you remember the feel of the tack, how the wind catches the sail, how to loosen it a little and then hold it back again, to go before the wind?'

'I remember all that.'

'And you?' he said to Cáit. 'What do you know?'

'I've never even held a rope, but I've been out in a *gleoiteog* and I could do whatever Barbara tells me.'

'Captain and crew, then. That's all you need.'

So he was not going to offer to come with us. I was not sure whether to be glad or sorry for this. The prospect of handling the boat alone was terrifying, but so was the thought of being cooped up in it, even for a few hours, with Mr Lennon. Any doubts I might have had were removed when he reached back into the cupboard behind him and took out a half-full bottle of whiskey. He had a glass ready on the dresser, also within reach, and he poured himself a measure and drank off half of it. We tried not to watch him but I don't think he cared.

'That's not all,' I said. 'We'll need to get to know the boat, somehow or other.'

'We can't go for a sail in her,' Cáit said anxiously. 'There would be ructions if either of us were seen going next or near a boat now.'

'You can have dry-land lessons,' Mr Lennon said. 'It won't be the same but after all it's not as if you had never sailed before. No one will interfere so long as you don't actually go on board.'

His idea was a good one, that he should go down to his boat every fine day after school and spend an hour or so cleaning her up and inspecting her sails. We would stay on the shore and watch, and he would give us some instruction about the different hazards we might have to deal with on our voyage. Mr Lennon's reputation for bad temper and bad manners would ensure that no one would come too near us, nor ask what we were doing.

'Then one day you can take the boat and sail her out, and no one can put the blame on me,' he said.

This was very important to us as well as to him. If the men thought that he had helped us to go, they might do some desperate thing in revenge before they could be stopped. If it seemed that we had stolen the boat, he could pretend to know nothing about us, and after a few days he could suggest that we might be found on the Island of Ghosts.

Of course we had many qualms of conscience in the next days, but we always returned to the same deadlock. Our choice was clear. It was out of the question to abandon the boys without a search, and yet we couldn't possibly announce our plan. We knew that our decision would hurt our parents still further, for a few days at least, but we saw no other way.

One thing was certain, that we could do nothing without Mr Lennon's help. We had our first lesson that very morning. He downed the rest of his drink and stood up saying:

'Come along, then. We mightn't get a day like this again for a while.'

We followed him out of the house and down to the shore.

'Sit on the rock, there, and let on that you're just idling the time away,' he said. 'Keep a sharp watch on everything I do.'

His boat was named *Naomh Éanna* after the Aran Island saint, who is of course one of our saints too. She was a beautiful boat, no more than twenty feet, built for pleasure, not for carrying cargo. Even her mast tapered off more elegantly than those they use in the *púcáns* that transport cattle and turf to and from the mainland. I found that I began to see things I had always taken for granted – that the lighter boat would be easier to handle for two greenhorns like us, that her high prow and swan-like tumble-home would save us from a lot of splashing and that her rudder was slender and looked easy to handle.

She was lying half in and half out of the water in the little cove below Mr Lennon's house, moored to two strong iron rings that were set in the rock above her. The half of her keel that rested on the sand was as clean as if he scrubbed it every day. When we arrived, a seagull was perched on the very top of the mast, surveying the calm sea in every direction. Another was preening his feathers, standing on the gunwale. Both flew off with wild cries, circling and hovering above us as if they would like to drive us off.

Mr Lennon clambered down on to the gunwale and untied the cords of the plastic covers. He folded them neatly and placed them carefully in the stern. Then he unlaced the cover of the sail and folded it away, and loosened the ropes that held it in position. Next we saw him haul up the sail in three long movements, the pulley turning with a crackling noise as the rope ran through. Everything he did was precise and exact. We watched, fascinated, wondering if we would ever achieve such skill and speed. Now that the sail was set at right-angles to the mast, the light wind filled it and the *gleoiteog* looked ready to take off for the wide ocean.

Sitting on our rock, with Bran snuggling between us, we began to feel the December air bite through our jerseys. Still Mr Lennon worked on, repeating the process of hauling up sail and letting it down again several times. He spoke no word to us, and we dared not speak to each other, no more than if we were at school.

Presently we became aware that first one man and then another and another had come over the top of the hill to watch what was happening. None of them stayed long, having concluded, I suppose, that Mr Lennon was just playing with his boat as he so often did. The tide was going out, and before he finished there was a shining patch of wet sand under the whole of the hull. Since it was quite clear that he was not going to put to sea, some of the men laughed among themselves as they turned to go home.

At last Mr Lennon stowed away the sail and replaced the covers on the boat. Then he climbed ashore and set off home. We followed him silently into his house and sat in our chairs again, for what seemed a long time, while he questioned us sharply about what we had learned.

When we reached home at dinner-time, we found that the story of how we had spent the morning had got there before us. My mother looked at me sadly and said:

'I don't like to see you going down to the shore, Barbara. The sea never did any good to me and mine. Let you stay up here with me now and I'll give you plenty to do around the house.'

'We were with Mr Lennon,' I said. 'He was teaching us things.'

'Mr Lennon and his teaching has us all ruined,' she said. 'God be with the days when no one had more learning than was needed to live their life long on the islands.'

'There was never such a day,' I said gently. 'Look at all the people that had to go across the ocean to America. They needed all the learning they could get.'

'It's true for you,' she said, 'and still I think the world has changed for the worse. But that's only because I'm getting old. Don't mind me, *a ghrá*. You have your own way of doing things, and sure Mr Lennon wants to do the best for you.'

But the sadness in her voice was like to break my heart. Instead of making me feel that we should give up our plan, it left me more determined than ever to go ahead with it and bring back the laughing and the fun that she always had until this terrible thing happened.

We had a few good days that December, then wild winds came roaring in from the Atlantic and thundered and crashed all around the island. Still we went several afternoons a week to Mr Lennon's house and listened while he explained the workings of sails and the way to handle a *gleoiteog* in reasonable weather.

'You can't go until the weather forecast is favourable,' he said. 'In a storm, even a good sailor would get into trouble. With two girls that hardly know a halliard from a sheet, the sea would eat you up in one bite. What's a halliard?'

He shot the question at me so suddenly that I nearly bit my tongue.

'The rope for hoisting the sail.'

'And a sheet?'

'The rope that angles the sail to the wind.'

'How do you reef the sail?'

'Ease off the throat halliard, then tighten the mainsheet and give it a turn around a thwart to hold it so that the boom won't swing over and knock you overboard.'

'What's the best place for the wind?'

'Abeam, then if the weather is good you can go by the wind.'

After an hour or so of this we could almost feel the sea heaving under us as we sat tensely on our kitchen chairs.

Mr Lennon's narrowed eyes and suspicious glare as we began our answers gave way after a while to grudging praise. Several times he said as we stood up to go:

'You'll soon be experts, on dry land at least. Heaven knows what you'll be like at sea.'

From him this was as good as saying that we would make first-rate sailors.

Christmas came and went, and it was a sad season in our house and in Cáit's. We found it hard to keep our secret to ourselves, though we knew that if we let out as much as a hint of what was in our minds, our plan would be finished.

January came in cold and dreary, with heaving seas and a north-east wind that seemed set to stay for good. Then gradually we noticed that the evenings were drawing out and the light was staying longer and longer. One Saturday morning in early February Mr Lennon said:

'Three fine days are all you need, one to go and one to come home, and a day in between. Any minute now we'll be promised them. Will you be ready?'

'Yes, of course we will,' I said, though I felt my inside sink at the thought of the two of us taking off alone.

We had talked a lot about the terrain of the Island of Ghosts, and the possibility of getting a good landfall there. Mr Lennon knew as little about it as we did, but he said that the people who lived there must have had some kind of safe harbour, else they couldn't have stayed there at all.

'Don't run her up on a sandy beach unless you're driven to it,' he said. 'The best would be to sail around the island until you see a cove or a harbour of some kind, and get yourselves safely in there, in good shelter. Then you'll be free to go ashore and find out if our idea is the right one.'

Neither of us could make any answer to that. At the thought that we might find the island deserted, many a time we had come near to despair. At last we had agreed not to speak of that possibility again. Mr Lennon stared at us for a moment, then went on to other things.

'Food,' he said. 'You'll need bread and eggs and milk enough to keep you going for a few days. I'll see to all of that, and you won't have to try to get the things at home. I'll leave them in the locker in the stern, the evening before. You'll go out on the high tide, so you won't need any help from me.' He stopped, still with that penetrating stare, then said: 'Are you quite sure you want to go?'

'What else would we do?' Cáit said angrily. 'We've thought of everything. If we managed to send for the Guards or the Army to go and search, they might arrest Mr Webb and put him in jail. That's not what we want at all, only to get the boys home safe and sound. Anyway, the Guards or the Army wouldn't listen to two girls, you know very well. And we'll be quite safe. We know all about sailing now.'

'All right, all right. I just wonder if I'll ever see God, after my part in this.'

If Mr Lennon were to weaken now, the whole plan would be finished. The sooner we went, the better. Both of us felt that we had learned as much of the theory of sailing as we ever would.

'Pray for a fine spell of weather soon,' I said on the way home that day, 'or he won't let us go at all.'

His doubts had shaken our confidence badly, though neither of us would admit it. Fortunately, a day or two later the radio weatherman announced that a long clear spell was on its way, with light south-westerly winds and long visibility. I heard it at home at four o'clock in the afternoon and went running down to tell Cáit. Together we set out for Mr Lennon's house.

We saw at once that he had heard it too. The bottle of whiskey was on the kitchen table this time, and he poured a fresh measure as we came in. Then he pushed the glass aside as if it had nothing to do with him and said:

'The time has come. The tide is right. High tide at six tomorrow morning. Will you be ready?'

'We're always ready.'

'God help us, I think you are. In all my life I never met a pair of little girls like you.'

We looked at our feet and said nothing. This remark could be dangerous, I thought, but in fact he didn't follow it up. From then on he was all practical advice. We had to go through our drill again, hoist the sail, cast off, steer out of the cove, set our course for the Island of Ghosts. This time we would be quite alone.

'I daren't go down to see you off,' he said. 'There's a fifty-fifty chance that someone will see you and get out his boat and follow you. They're all such good sailors, they would be sure to overhaul you. If that happens, you can do nothing but turn back.'

'We won't turn back for anyone. If they want to, they can follow us all the way.'

Chapter Eleven

NO ONE ON INISHGLASS GETS UP EARLY. I don't know why this is so, since one would think that people who have so much work to do would be eager to get started at the crack of dawn. Perhaps the reason is that everyone loves company and chat and talk, so that people don't go to bed early either. When the fire is blazing and the kettle singing and the talk gets better and better, no one wants to be the first to break it up and go home.

Whatever the reason, at six o'clock next morning Cáit and I were the only people stirring on the island. All night long I had been restless, waking every few hours in a panic lest I had slept too long. The first chirpings from the hens told me the time. I slid out of bed like a shadow. Bran lifted his head as soon as I went into the kitchen, then followed me silently outside, close behind my heels, as if he knew there was to be no barking today. The dawn air was crisp and clean, so that the first pull of it into my lungs sent a shiver of excitement through me.

I was in a cold sweat until I found Cáit waiting for me at the turn of the road below her house. Nellie Mór was as tender as a cat about every move that was made, and if she had woken up we would have been done for.

Running on the grass by the roadside we made no sound. There was scarcely a ripple on the sea. At that hour in February there is a sort of half-light, purple and grey shading to pink on the horizon where the sun is hiding. A faint dark curve in the distance was the Island of Ghosts, visible today for the first time in weeks.

'I wish Mr Lennon would come down and help us off,' Cáit said. 'It's a lonesome way to go.'

I said nothing, though I was thinking the same thing. We knew that it was better to go independently but now all our lessons seemed useless. Silently we went over them as we climbed aboard the *gleoiteog*, following all the instructions we had been given so often, hauling up sail, casting off, feeling a moment of pure terror as the boat moved away from the quay and took to the sea like a bird. She made a tiny rippling sound at the bows, a warm, comfortable sound as if she knew what she was doing, and this gave us more comfort than any of our remembered knowledge. Even Bran, who had crawled into the stern and lay there watching us nervously, came out and sat amidships looking around him as if he were enjoying himself.

'There's nothing to sailing, after all,' I said when we were well away from the shore. 'Why do they make such a fuss about it?'

'Nothing to it on a calm sea,' Cáit said. 'I hope the weatherman is right.'

She stood at the helm and I took care of the sail. It was exactly as Mr Lennon had said – when you got the feel of the wind you were guided by instinct as much as by knowledge. Besides, Cáit and I knew each other so well that we could each sense what the other was thinking. Now I understood why the men always sailed with the same partners, since knowing each other's ways was half the skill.

Out from Inishglass, we kept looking back anxiously for signs of life there, people running to the shore and pointing after us, as they would surely have done if anyone had seen us go. But there was no one. Not even a hint of smoke went up from any of the houses. Everyone except ourselves was fast asleep.

'Lazybones, the whole lot of them,' Cáit said. 'This is the best time of the day.'

'If anyone gets up now and sees the boat,' I said, 'even if they recognize it, they'll just think Mr Lennon has gone out for a sail.'

We had had no breakfast, and were suddenly mad with hunger. Cáit opened the locker and brought out some of the bread and eggs that he had left. There was a scribbled note, too, obviously written at the last moment as if he had doubts about letting us out at all. We read it as we ate:

Don't try to reef the sail unless you must.

Allow fifty yards to get to your moorings after you lower the sail.

Don't let the boat come up into the wind.

Keep your sail full and your boat moving.

Good luck!

We were both silent for a while, thinking of him, how good he had been to us, how much time he had given us and above all that he had lent us his beloved boat. Then I said:

'I wonder what he was like when he was a boy. I wonder if he played with other boys, football and hurling and handball, or with girls.'

'My grandmother says he's a changeling,' said Cáit. 'She says the fairies left him instead of a baby they fancied, when he was small. One thing is sure, he's not like any real person I ever knew. He'll never be different.'

Still I was sorry for him and wished he could be more likeable. The worst was that just when you were beginning to trust him, he would turn on you and snarl and bark like a cross dog. No one could make friends with a person like that.

As the sun rose higher and higher, the sea glowed with a strong white light, reflecting the high white clouds. The boat climbed the long, slow waves easily, in a gentle rhythm. As we tacked towards the Island of Ghosts, at first it seemed to move farther and farther away, just as Hy-Breasail was said to do. Then gradually it turned a dark, patchy green, and little by little its real colours showed.

Neither of us spoke as we watched the land come closer. There was no sign of life there, that we could see, only a long sandy beach with a high ridge above, and rocks at one end. Beyond that the island rose to a cliff, dropping straight into the sea as if it had been cut off with a knife.

And there was the great sweep of grassland that Mr Webb had praised. I had imagined it as one huge pasture, but now we saw that there were walled fields, bathed in sunlight, and a little grove of trees at one end. Most wonderful of all was that here and there in the fields we could see small animals grazing. At first we couldn't make out what they were, then I said:

'Goats and sheep, of course. He said they could live there.'

Then, at the same moment we both shouted:

'Smoke!'

There was no doubt whatever about it. Up from among the trees, a wandering feather of smoke fluttered and was blown away by the wind. In my excitement I almost let go of the sheet and the boat heeled over. Cáit righted it with a quick pull on the helm, then said,

'Let's not sink within sight of land.'

But she was nearly crying with excitement too. Neither of us could think clearly as we came closer and closer to the land, our heads were such a jumble of mixed-up sensations.

'He said not to run her up on the strand,' I said. 'Then where do we go?'

'Around the tip, I suppose.'

The sandy beach lay along the westward end of the island as far as we could see, and beyond that there were only the black rocks, which looked jagged and threatening. We sailed along the length of the strand, perhaps a quarter of a mile offshore, until we were level with these rocks, watching out for some kind of a harbour. There was none, though a cleft between two of them looked as if it might allow the passage of the boat. But what would we do if it didn't? That would be worse than running aground on the beach.

Suddenly Cáit gave a kind of scream:

'There they are!'

All the breath left my lungs. Two figures were standing on the highest point, to one side of the cleft. They were waving their arms and pointing, then one of them ran a little way and came back, waving again, so that there was no mistaking what he meant. They were still so far away that we couldn't recognize either of them. In any case, lowering the sail and steering the boat between the rocks took up all our attention, until we came almost to the moment of entering the harbour.

That was what it was, a long fiord like the one below Mr Webb's house on Inishglass. And there was Mr Webb himself, and my brother Dara, both shouting directions to us, almost dancing up and down as they pointed and waved. Cáit handled the helm as if she had been doing it all her life and the *gleoiteog* slid silently along until Mr Webb was able to lean down and grasp her gunwale. Then I threw him a rope and he tied us up neatly to an iron ring set in the rock.

Then I looked up into Dara's face and asked:

'Where is Brendan?'

'At the house.'

We said no more after that until we had climbed ashore. First I handed up Bran, who was squeaking with excitement at seeing Dara again. That was a great reunion. Bran licked his face and neck over and over, as if he had to make sure that the taste was right. When we leaned across to hug him, we got a powerful lick too. Then we stood looking down into the *gleoiteog*.

'That's Mr Lennon's boat,' Dara said. 'How did you manage to get it?'

'He lent it to us.'

In Mr Webb's presence I would say no more, and I was glad that Dara didn't question us any further. He looked very well and healthy, as if he had been eating the best of good food every day since leaving home. From what we had always heard of the Island of Ghosts, we wouldn't have been surprised to have found three skeletons. Cáit asked:

'Why is Brendan not here? Is he sick?'

'He had an accident – he broke his leg, but Mr Webb fixed it and he's getting better.'

Both of us knew that look on Dara's face, a blank stare like a dog. As clear as daylight it said: 'Don't say any more about that. We can talk about it later.'

Mr Webb was saying heartily:

'You're a great pair of sailors. I never knew that island girls could sail a boat.'

'They can when they need to,' I said.

'Well, now that you're here, come up to the house. We have dozens of things to show you.'

'Is the boat safe?'

'In this weather, yes, but we lost our boat a long time ago and we've been marooned here every since. You'll see that we did very well. Isn't that so, Dara?'

'Indeed it is.'

Mr Webb sprang ahead of us at great speed, and we followed in single file, with Bran staying close to Dara. Once Dara turned and gazed at us, shaking his head slightly, then putting one finger first on his lips and then against his temple. We understood at once. We were not to speak, and he was suggesting that Mr Webb was touched in the head. He didn't look any different to us from what he was in Inishglass, though it was certainly odd that he had shown no signs of surprise at our arrival. It was almost as if he had been expecting us. And he hadn't asked after our families, nor even seemed to think that Dara should do so.

When we came up from the narrow path that led from the cove, there was no more chance of using sign language. Now we all walked together, Mr Webb making us stop now and then while he showed off the wonders of his island. He was specially proud of the stream, where he planned to fix a little machine to generate electricity.

'I'll show you how that will be done,' he said cheerfully. 'How to repair it too. It's very important to know how to do your own repairs. At present this pumps water to the house and to the animals' watering-troughs. Dara is an expert on waterworks now.'

A flock of sheep was grazing, scattered over a long green pasture. We had to stop and admire them.

'We have thirty-nine lambs,' he said. 'We're making a spinning-wheel and a loom, so that we can weave our own wool, and of course we'll have cheese and meat as well. But we don't eat much meat. I'm not sure that man was meant to eat meat at all. Bran can have a new job now – Dara says he's good with sheep.'

Cáit and I dared not look at each other. Fortunately he didn't expect an answer. At last the house had come in view and he was leading us towards it.

'It's wonderful what one can do in a few months. Dara will tell you that I had done a great many things before he and Brendan came, but we did a lot more during the winter. Now with the longer evenings we have much more time. You know, we were working at the reservoir, up on the ridge, when we saw you coming. There's a tremendous view over the sea. We often saw Inishglass, on a fine day. We should go up there at once, so that you can get a look at the whole island in perspective.'

And he actually turned aside as if he were going to climb the ridge.

Suddenly Cáit lost her patience.

'Mr Webb,' she said, 'I want to see my brother. Where is he?'

'Ah yes, your brother. Of course. He's in the house, I suppose, where we left him.'

I thought Cáit would run at him and thump him with her fists. She never was a patient girl, and this time she had had more than she could stand.

'Let's go inside first and talk to Brendan,' I said quickly. 'We've come a long way to see him.'

'Very well. Yes.'

For a moment I thought he would let us go in alone but there was no hope of that. Again he led the way, through the beautiful little front garden. A leafless rose-tree was trained against the house wall. It was all as neat as a new pin, though no flowers were blooming there at this time of the year.

The door stood open so that we could see into the kitchen. Bran ran in ahead of us, and Mr Webb called out:

'Brendan! Some visitors!'

He had been sitting in a high-backed chair by the fire, a pair of heavy wooden crutches lying on the floor beside him. He got up slowly, helping himself with the arms of the chair, and stood there, looking at us in astonishment. Both of us ran to him, then stopped, afraid to hug him lest we might knock him down. He put out his arms unsteadily, then sat down carefully while we knelt beside him, burying our heads in his lap. Cáit was crying, whether with rage or pity I couldn't tell. He looked over her head at me, and said softly:

'I dreamed of you last night, that you would manage to come somehow, that someone would give you a boat.'

Mr Webb was hovering close to us, obviously not wanting to miss a word.

'Brendan has strange dreams,' he said, in a contemptuous tone. 'Now here's one that has come true.'

Chapter Twelve

BRENDAN AND THE TWO GIRLS have said that I must get on with the story. That bright spring evening, I was working with Bardal up on the ridge of the island. I stood up to stretch my back and saw the *gleoiteog* sailing straight towards us.

I had seen island boats several times since we had come to the island, but always in the distance. There had been no possibility whatever of waving to them, even if Bardal hadn't kept such a close watch on us. Besides, I knew very well that if I had waved, the boat would have made off at speed. Our surest jailor was the reputation of the island.

A strange thing had happened to me in the months since we had been on the Island of Ghosts. Very gradually, as the months passed, I had come to love it. It was lonesome with only the three of us, I was there against my will, I knew we must be mourned for dead on Inishglass – and yet I found that Bardal's ingenuity, the things he had invented and carried through, especially the success of his sheep-farming and of his goats, all filled me with such admiration that I began to find our life there almost pleasant.

Brendan's broken leg was very slow in healing and he was confined to the house most of the time, reading the books that Bardal assigned to him, making the bread and doing any housework that he could manage. We had made him a pair of rough crutches and he hobbled around on these as best as he could. He had no sympathy with my feelings.

'We might as well be in a concentration camp,' he said bitterly. 'He even carries that little radio of his in his pocket, so that we won't find out what's going on in the outside world. I don't know how you can find a good word to say for him.'

I tried to talk about the beauties of the place, the grassy pasture, the perfect little house, the high windy ridge from which you could see for miles and miles on a clear day, the pleasure of coming home in the evening to cook a good meal, then rest and read, and sleep at last as one only does after a hard day's work. But it was no use. Brendan looked at me as if I were crazy, and made no answer.

Bardal sensed that I had come to believe in his dream,

but naturally after what we had done to him, he never trusted me. He never left me alone in any position where I might have engineered our escape, never by the cove even after our boat disappeared, though he knew there was nothing whatever I could do without it. Besides, he knew that I wouldn't leave Brendan, and that even if I had a boat it would be impossible to take him with me in his present condition.

Brendan was miserable at being an invalid. He had never liked Bardal as much as I did, and had always wondered why he put himself out so much for us, teaching us so that we won the scholarships, continuing to teach us still, whenever he had an hour or two to spare. He always took special care that Brendan had something to learn, so that he wouldn't be bored when we were out, as we often were, for a few hours at a time.

Our only chance to talk privately was when we lay in bed in our room off the kitchen.

'You shouldn't be so suspicious,' I said one night after Christmas. 'Bardal is teaching us out of the goodness of his heart. That's how he sees it.'

'He sees that he can make use of us. He had it all planned. He wanted to live here but he was afraid to come alone. Now he wants to make excuses for what he did to us.'

'He's not afraid of anything,' I protested.

'He's afraid of being alone,' Brendan said positively. 'He thinks it's a weakness and he'll never say it, but you can see it by everything he does. He always wants you to be with him, and when he's at home he's chatting to me about Latin and Greek –'

'That's because he's sorry for you,' I said. 'He knows you're bored sitting there all day with your books, waiting for your leg to mend. He doesn't want you to waste your time.'

'He's afraid of the ghosts.'

'What ghosts?'

'The woman in the long skirt. Don't pretend you haven't seen her. And you must have heard the child crying.'

'Yes. I've heard it, and I've seen her, but I thought you hadn't.'

'When did you see her?'

'The first evening, when I went out for the turf.'

'In a long black skirt, with her hair up?'

'Yes.'

'Were you afraid?'

'Terrified, though I could see she meant me no harm. It was really that I was sorry for her.'

'And since then?'

'Sometimes,' I admitted. 'She came the evening you broke your leg. She stood looking down at you, when you had fainted. I think she just came to have a look at you, as she did with me.'

'Did he see her that time?'

'If he did, he made no sign of it.'

'When both of you are out of the house, she comes and stands near me, only for a few seconds. I think this was her house.'

'Yes, it was. Bardal says it was the only house on the island.' I hesitated to ask the next question but it had been on my mind so long that I went ahead. 'What about the man? Have you seen him?'

'What man?'

'The woman's husband. He died here too. Have you seen him?'

'Never. Have you?'

'No. There must have been other children too.'

'There were three older ones, and her brother. Does she speak to you?' Brendan asked.

'No,' I said, 'but she has only stayed for a few moments.'

'She doesn't speak to me either. But I often have dreams about her.'

'What are the dreams?'

'About her life here, and the way they got the fever, and no one came, and the baby cried and cried and she could do nothing for it.' He stopped suddenly. 'I can't talk about it. You know what happened.'

'Does she speak in your dreams?'

'Not exactly. It's more like a story that comes into my head.'

'And you think Bardal sees her too? What would she have to say to him?'

'Nothing. I think she's angry with him because he brought us here, and still she's glad to have us, to have people come to live here again.'

'That's a good dream to have.'

'You don't believe me,' he said, 'or you think I'm going out of my mind. I tell you, it happens. And she gave me the idea that we'll have a visit soon, from home. I can't ask her any questions. I can only wait for what she puts into my mind.'

The next evening I got Bardal talking about dreams. We were sitting over the last of dinner when I asked him suddenly, 'Do you believe in second sight?'

I had hoped to surprise a quick answer from him but he smiled in an odd way and said:

'Why do you ask?'

I could see that Brendan was getting uneasy, sending

me warning looks, but I went on anyway:

'A few of the old people on Inishglass are said to have it.'

'I never knew anyone who did. Perhaps it's just wishful thinking.'

'It can't be that. Sometimes they foretold terrible disasters, like the time all the boats were lost with the big wave. There was no talk of a storm coming, and still an old woman named Mag Colm said they should stay home. She went down to the shore, crying after them as if they were drowned already. None of them ever came back.'

'Did you see that happening?'

'No. It happened before I was born. But I've heard talk of it all my life.'

'I'd have to see it before I'd believe it. Brendan would be the one for dreams, not you,' he said. 'Isn't that so, Brendan?'

'I dream of strange things, all right,' he said.

'Of what?'

'Of the people that used to live here long ago, that can't lie easy.'

'Well, they were your relatives,' Bardal said seriously. 'It's no wonder you dream of them. Why don't they lie easy?'

'I suppose they never got decent burial.'

'We can't do anything for them now.' Suddenly he was no longer calmly smiling at our simplicity. 'That's enough of that talk. Forget it, do you hear?'

When he used that tone, neither of us dared to disobey. I never talked to him of such things again, and Brendan and I never spoke of the ghostly woman, though we both saw her from time to time.

The day that the girls sailed in, at first I thought that Bardal hadn't noticed the *gleoiteog*. We were digging out the reservoir, which according to his plan was to take the water from the second well, high up in that windy place. There were times when I thought I would die of cold. Skinny as he was, Bardal never seemed to suffer as I did.

The reservoir was to be joined, by a little canal, to the stream as it tumbled downhill. He never tired of explaining how exact the measurements had to be, to make sure that the inward and outward flow would be controlled so that the reservoir would never spill over. This was very interesting, indeed, but I had so many anxieties that I couldn't give it my whole attention. No matter how much I learned, half of my mind was always on other things.

My back ached miserably and my hands were sore with handling the shovel. I had straightened up to ease my muscles for a moment, expecting that his cheerful voice would call out:

'On with the work! No slacking now that we're in sight of the end!'

Instead, without lifting his head Bardal said:

'Here they come. They've been a long time.'

'You knew they were coming?' I was stammering in my amazement.

'Not exactly, but I thought it likely that you wouldn't be forgotten too easily.' Then he laughed in that infuriating way he had and said: 'Work it out for yourself. You should know better than anyone. Perhaps Brendan dreamed of it.'

It was no use trying to get any more out of him. I had learned that by experience. We worked on for a quarter of an hour before he said:

'I think we can go down to the cove now. They'll need help to get in.'

I ran ahead of him, sick of the calm way he was talking. I was up on the rocks, waving and yelling, minutes before he arrived. I couldn't make out the people in the boat, they were so small. Boys, perhaps – it never occurred to me that they could be girls, especially our girls. Then I heard Bardal at my elbow say quietly:

'Barbara and Cáit, of course. Can't you see them?'

As they came closer I recognized them, the dark head and the fair one, concealed now and then by the movement of the huge sail. How they had learned to manage a boat I couldn't imagine, nor how they would get into the tiny harbour without wrecking themselves.

'They'll do it,' Bardal said. 'The tide is perfect.'

And he raced out to the highest point and began to wave them in, calling directions in a voice that must have carried a mile, like a seagull's cry. I did my share of waving too, and they steered into the tricky little harbour as if they had been doing it every day of the week. They threw a rope ashore and Bardal made it fast to the ring. By this time Bran had seen me and was springing hysterically from side to side of the boat. When Barbara handed him up to me, I could feel his heart beating fit to burst, under my hands.

I had only one or two chances of warning the girls to be careful what they said in front of Bardal, but they took my hints immediately. He treated them as if they had suffered no anxiety on our account, though he had lived long enough on Inishglass to know that when someone disappears at sea, the mourning goes on for months. He actually wanted them to see the wonders of his island before going to the house. It was my Cáit that stood up to him and demanded to be brought to her brother at once.

Bardal agreed, of course. I'll pass over the pain of the meeting between the girls and Brendan. Bardal watched them impatiently but afterwards we had to make the full tour of his wonders, including the cheese-shed and the hen-house, before he asked them if they were hungry.

'Famished,' Barbara said at once. 'We brought plenty of food with us but in the end we forgot to eat it.'

Poor Brendan had had to stay behind, of course. Bardal wouldn't even leave him Bran for company and he limped to the door on his crutches to see us go. Barbara turned several times to wave to him. I knew she was counting the moments until we could get back to him, but once Bardal got started on describing his great plans, there was no stopping him. At last he turned reluctantly for home.

The days that followed would have been a pure joy, if only we could have had time alone, to talk at our ease and tell all the things that had happened since our last meeting and to hear their news of home. The two girls slept in the room beside Bardal's, so that we had no chance of slipping in to talk to them during the night, nor for them to come to us. Often Barbara stayed at the house with Brendan while Cáit came with me to help with all my jobs. After the first day Bardal allowed this – in fact he seemed rather pleased with it – but he would never consent to leaving the four of us alone together.

When we wanted to ask about our parents and what had happened after we disappeared, it had to be around the table after supper. That first evening, we told them about the fierce storm that had washed the *gleoiteog* out of the cove, and how Bardal and Brendan and I had watched from the top of the cliff as it went spinning off under bare poles. In Bardal's presence I couldn't describe our despair.

'Then it really was your boat that was lost,' Barbara said. 'We would never believe it, though everyone else did.'

Bardal let us go on for a while, then he said impatiently:

'That's enough of that. No use in crying over spilt milk. Time for a game of Scrabble.'

Brendan had long ago absolutely refused to play, and Bardal was nearly always able to beat me at the game. Now I got great satisfaction out of seeing how Cáit was well able for him. She didn't often win, of course, but she forced him to bring out his strongest skill in a way he never had to do with me. And he seemed delighted with this. When Cáit stared at the board for a few minutes, considering her move, he would say:

'Take your time. No hurry. Do the very best you can.'

Then he would watch her with a sparkle in his eyes, like a man watching a good sheep-dog. When Cáit won a game, she would laugh with pleasure and then explain how she had done it, and how he could improve his game by using some of her methods.

I was very pleased to see them making friends, since Brendan by now would scarcely speak to him. Barbara was more civil. Indeed on the outside one would think she was just as friendly as Cáit. But when we got a chance to be alone together she always said:

'We must get away soon. The moment that Brendan is fit to move, we'll have to be off.'

'He won't allow it.'

'We'll have to deal with that when the time comes.'

The good spring weather continued, with a calm blue sea and a clear sky showing no sign of change to come. Now and then I got a chance to run down to the cove and see that the boat was safe. I would make sure that Bardal and Cáit were doing something that would keep them occupied for a while. Turning the cheese trays was a good chance. This had to be done regularly, and there was only room for two in the little shed.

The boat lay there, quite safe, rising and falling with the tide. Her rudder was made in such a way that it couldn't be easily removed, and this time Bardal had not been able to take it away. We knew from the girls that some day soon a rescue party would arrive. Then we would simply have to get aboard her and haul up sail and make for home, leaving him behind.

The thought filled me with sadness and a feeling of shame at treating him so badly, after all he had done for us. I knew that I had learned more from him in the months we had lived together than I would have learned in years of boarding-school. The idea of going back to begin on that shut-in life tightened my stomach and made my head ache.

It was on the way back from one of these expeditions that I found the answer. As I climbed up from the cove, there came Cáit running towards me. Her long bright hair was flying out behind her and her bare feet flashed like snow against the green grass. I stood still and waited for her, and caught her quickly as she ran into my arms. Then I said, looking down at her, still holding her tightly:

'Cáit, when we're older and when they let us get married, would you live here with me on the Island of Ghosts?'

'Of course I would,' she said, 'but we'll have to give it another name.'

'That will be easy.'

When we reached the house, the other three were in

the kitchen. Barbara was helping Brendan to walk up and down, as she did every day. He looked almost cheerful, leaning his right hand on her shoulder and holding one crutch in his left.

'Look!' she said. 'Soon he'll be able to walk by himself.'

'You see,' Bardal said easily, 'everything comes right on Hy-Breasail. Now we can all live happily together forever.'

Chapter Thirteen

MR LENNON HAS REFUSED to tell the rest of the story, though it concerns him as much as any of us, perhaps more.

'I can do figures until they come out through my ears,' he said testily when I asked him, 'but I have no skill with words. I leave that to you and the little girls. Wasn't your grandfather a song-maker and a poet?'

Whatever about that, telling the end of the story fell to me. It was not easy to piece it together from what I was told, both by my mother and by Mr Lennon, but at last I believe I heard everything.

Mr Lennon had expected the girls to be away for three days, as he had said. On the evening of the first day, when it was found that they had disappeared, with the boat, the whole of Inishglass was in an uproar. The Galway lifeboat was called out, of course, and it cruised the waters of the Bay from side to side in search of the wreckage. No one went to bed that night, as message after message came in that there was neither trace nor tidings of the boat, nor of its passengers.

The lifeboat Captain was astonished at the whole affair.

'Why did you let them go?' he asked sadly. 'Girls! It would take them to lose a boat in a flat calm – I don't understand how they managed it.'

No one answered him, and he went away convinced that the islanders were all fools. You may be sure they were not pleased at this but they could do nothing to defend themselves.

Still Mr Lennon held his tongue. Everyone knew that the girls had gone off in his boat. No one suspected that he had lent it to them, or had anything to do with their departure. Indeed our parents were full of sympathy for him, even in the midst of their own sorrow. My father and Bartley Conneeley, Brendan's father, said this when they went to his house to talk to him, and to invite him to come to the big wake that was being held for the girls on the second night.

'Don't we know what you must be feeling?' my father said. 'How can you blame yourself? What can two girls know about how to handle a boat? They must have been desperate, to do a crazy thing like that.'

Mr Lennon made no answer except to say that he

would not go to the wake. He spoke in a loud, hard voice, so that my father was shocked.

'Aren't you our friend, that taught all our children? No one will say a word to you as long as they know we invited you.'

From this Mr Lennon guessed that there was indeed some talk of his part in the tragedy and he was afraid to risk being questioned. Time enough for that when the *gleoiteog* would come sailing back to her anchorage below his house. Being so sure that this would happen, he didn't look as sad as he should and the two men went away puzzled and upset.

At the wake, Maggie Cooney came out with her usual brand of mischief.

'And where is the schoolmaster?' she demanded in a loud voice. 'Wouldn't you think he'd be here with the rest of us, doing his share of crying and praying for the dead?'

'He's not coming,' Bartley Conneeley said. 'I think he's too sad for company. You know he's like a father to all the children in the school.'

Maggie snorted.

'I wouldn't be wanting a father like that,' she said. 'He's a hard-hearted man, that he wouldn't come and sit by the side of the real fathers, and give them a bit of comfort.'

There were a few murmurs of agreement. It stopped when my mother came into the kitchen. Sarah Kane hushed Maggie up and hissed to everyone that they should be quiet and not add to the pain of the poor mother with that kind of talk.

Two more days passed, while Mr Lennon watched and waited for the boat to come. After school he would sit on the rocks above his little harbour, wrapped in his old black coat, gazing out to sea so as not to miss the first sight of it by as much as a second. My father found him like this on the third evening and stood silently beside him. Darkness was falling and shadows were sliding over the sea from the horizon. There was a bitter little wind, which nipped at them even through their heavy clothes.

'It's no use, old friend,' my father said after a long pause. 'We must accept the will of God. There is some terrible need in Him to take away our children one by one.'

Mr Lennon couldn't bear to deceive him any longer.

'They're on the Island of Ghosts,' he said. 'They've gone to find the boys and bring them back. Any moment now they'll come in sight. Keep your eyes on the sea –'

'We know you feel the pain as bad as ourselves,' my father said gently, 'but we're gone past hope now. It's better to get used to it.'

And he gave him a look that said plainly that he thought Mr Lennon had lost his wits. Soon afterwards it was clear that the whole island had the same opinion. At school the children watched his gloomy face silently, so that he knew he was the subject of talk in all their houses. Still he sat looking out to sea every evening, until he himself began to think that the people were right, and that he would never again lay eyes on the girls nor on his boat.

When they had been gone for six days, as he sat in his usual place on the cold rock my father came up behind him and touched him on the shoulder.

'Come down with me now, Master, and sit by the fire in our house,' he said. 'You're too long watching.' Mr Lennon turned to him with such a strange look in his eyes that my father grabbed him tightly and said, 'Man, you're sick. Stand up and come with me.'

'I must wait for them,' Mr Lennon said hoarsely. 'They'll be back, any moment now. Look – there they are!'

He waved his arms wildly towards the darkening sky. He told me himself that in his fever he really believed he saw the boat at that moment, sailing towards him through the air.

Somehow my father got him down from the rock and brought him to his house, where he laid him on his bed and ran to fetch my mother. Distracted with grief as she was, still she went to him at once. In no time she had set my father to build a fire and warm the place, which was as cold as a tomb. Together they got him into bed and she began her usual series of cures for men who had been out at sea too long – hot soup with poteen in it, hot milk with beaten-up eggs, regular doses of aspirin, above all a blazing fire.

Worse than any amount of nursing, she told me afterwards, was listening to him rambling on about the boys who were safe on the Island of Ghosts, and who would be home with the girls any day now. It was no use trying to stop him, since he seemed not to hear her when she spoke to him.

He was at this late one evening when my Aunt Kate came into the house. She had come to spend the night with the patient, as she had done every night since his illness, sending my mother home to sleep when he seemed to be quieter. She listened for a minute or two, then said sharply:

'I never heard him talk like that before. Barbara, God rest her, said the same thing to me on the night of the wake for the boys. I told her it was nonsense.'

'You never told me.'

'How could I, and you out of your mind with the loss of

your own boy? Listen to him.'

They listened, and heard him muttering over and over, instructions about handling the boat.

'Fifty yards to get to your moorings – don't let her into the wind – don't reef – a few lessons and you think you know it all – not enough – keep her full –' There was a pause and then he tried to sit up in the bed, saying loudly:

'Here they come! A sweet boat – sails by herself –'

He smiled happily and fell back into a deep sleep.

The two women moved into the kitchen.

'You see,' Aunt Kate said quietly. 'It's as clear as daylight. My guess is that the girls asked him to help them to get to the boys. He gave them the boat and told them how to manage her, and sent them off. If the men hear this, they'll kill him for sure. Bartley Conneeley has a short temper.'

'Then what can we do?'

'You can tell Tomás what we've just heard and he'll know how to talk to Bartley. They're great friends. It would be hard for Bartley to go against Tomás.'

'That's true,' my mother said. 'One thing is certain – Tomás wouldn't be afraid to go to the Island of Ghosts. He often told me that it's nonsense to believe in a place being cursed. He wouldn't say it to anyone else because he doesn't want to make bad friends. A postmaster has to be good friends with everyone.'

In the minds of both of them was the fear that their idea was far-fetched, and that they would only create false hopes in the two fathers. At last Kate said:

'Fetch Tomás, then, and let him hear for himself.'

He came, and waited until Mr Lennon stirred and began to ramble again, always about the Island of Ghosts and his sweet boat that would soon come sailing home. My father listened for a while, then said, 'God forgive him, you'd think he cares more about his old boat than about the children in it. He was always a strange man. But there's no doubt about what he's saying. He believes that his boat has gone to the Island of Ghosts. If that's true, then we can do no better than to follow her.'

Aunt Kate stayed with Mr Lennon and my parents went home to talk over what to do next. Bartley Conneeley had to be told at once, of course, but my father agreed that it would be dangerous to let him know about Mr Lennon's part in the business. They would have to keep Bartley away from him until he returned to his senses.

The first thing was to get Bartley away for a quiet talk, but by this time it was almost midnight. There was a long wait until the morning but they had to endure it. At eight o'clock, the earliest they thought was reasonable, my mother walked down to Conneeley's house to fetch Bartley. She saw at once that there was no hope of going inside to have a talk with his wife. Nellie Mór was there, on the watch as usual, pretending to be at work in the cabbage-garden by the door.

'What do you want with him?' she asked at once, guessing that something interesting was afoot.

'Tomás wants to have a few words with him,' my mother said innocently.

'Why didn't he come down himself?'

'He has to mind the telegraph. Where is Bartley?'

'Up in the high field, milking,' Nellie said reluctantly.

So they were able to talk without being overheard by anyone except the cows. By good luck the milking was finished. When he heard that Tomás had an idea that we might be safe, Bartley let out such a shout that the cows went galloping off up the field. My mother calmed him down somehow and walked with him to our house, carrying one of his cans of milk. All the way there he pelted her with questions, so that she almost had to run to keep ahead of him.

'You'll hear,' she said over and over. 'Tomás will tell you.'

In the quiet of our kitchen my father made him sit at

the table while my mother made a pot of tea. They refused to tell him anything more until they were sure he was steady enough to take it in, but my mother said it was pitiful to watch him shift his big, sad eyes from one of them to the other.

'We think they could all be on the Island of Ghosts,' my father said at last.

'What gives you that idea? Why should they be there? What would take them out to that place? Do you mean that they're all there, all four of them?'

'They could be.'

'How do you know? Who told you this? Who sent them there? If I knew who it was, I'd kill him in his tracks.'

Bartley leaped to his feet with a murderous look, his fists clenched.

'Sit down,' my father said. 'Who said that anyone sent them? If you can't be quiet and give up that kind of talk, I won't tell you any more.'

He sat down, shivering as if he were cold, though there was a big fire blazing on the hearth.

'I'll be quiet,' he said. 'What makes you think they might be on the Island of Ghosts?'

'A sort of message came.'

'On the telegraph?'

'As good as the telegraph. We must go there at once.'

'To that terrible place?'

'Would you be afraid? It belonged to your own people once.'

'You know very well that I'd cross the Atlantic Ocean if I thought I could get back my two chickens.'

Neither of them had mentioned Mr Webb. My mother had often tried to work out what was his part in the business. When it was discovered that his house was empty of furniture and of all his goods and chattels, the people had guessed rightly that he had got the boys to help him with his moving, and that this was why they had gone with him on the day of the storm. Bitter words were spoken about him, though his soul was prayed for with the others. He should have asked the men to help him, not a couple of boys. No one even bothered to find out where he had meant to live. For a long time now, his name was never said. It was as if he had never lived on Inishglass. They felt that they should never have trusted a foreigner and that they had only themselves to blame.

My mother had always had a soft spot for Bardal, as I've said. When Bartley went home, to tell his wife that there was some hope at last, she said,

'You know we may find Bardal there too.'

'I do know it,' my father said. 'I'll have to get every

man that comes with us to swear obedience as if he were in the army. It's the only way to protect him. Did you see the carry-on of Bartley? If we don't watch out, we'll have murder on our hands.'

Two boats would have to go, enough to deal with whatever they would find on the Island of Ghosts. My father would take Bartley in his boat, to keep an eye on him, with Seán Black and Cumeen Peter. Colie Joyce could take his own boat with three more, making eight in all, a useful army.

While my father went to find the men and try to persuade them to agree to all of this, my mother went to send Aunt Kate home for a sleep and to see how Mr Lennon was getting on. She found him sitting up in bed, pale as the sheet that he had pulled right up to his chin. When she opened the door he turned his usual baleful glare towards it, until he saw who it was that had come to visit him. Then his expression softened and he said,

'Your sister tells me that I've been away with the fairies for a few days. I think I was rambling in my talk.'

'You were, indeed,' my mother said. 'You're back in this world again, by the looks of you.'

'What did I say? Your sister wouldn't tell me.'

'You said plenty, enough to send two boat-loads out to the Island of Ghosts. And now you must say no more. If anyone asks any questions, you know nothing – nothing at all.'

He gave her a long look, then said, 'I'll do whatever you tell me.'

It took all day for my father to collect his two crews. Then it was too late for them to sail. Everything had to be explained to the men before they would agree to come, and each had to swear by his father and grandfather that he would not tell anyone what they were doing, and that he would obey orders like a soldier.

My father went first to Colie Joyce. By good luck he found him alone, working on his boat, doing a bit of caulking at the low tide. He had to repeat his story over and over before Colie took in what he was being asked to do.

'You know what they say about that place,' he said at last, 'that if you land on it you might never be able to get off it again with your life.'

'That's pagan talk. And there will be two boats with eight men.'

'I wouldn't do it for anyone else in the whole wide world. You have reason to think they're there?'

'Good reason.'

Somehow they managed to keep the secret, so that even Nellie Mór didn't know what was going on. She scented something, of course. She didn't dare to question Bartley but she dropped in to see my mother at five o'clock and settled down with a mug of tea by the fire. Soon she was asking,

'Why is Tomás going the rounds of all the houses? Everywhere I look, there he is walking up and down instead of minding his telegraph. There could be a world war starting and we none the wiser.'

'If there's a world war, we'll find out soon enough,' my mother said.

'But don't you know?'

'He knows himself, and that's enough for me.'

'It wouldn't be enough for me,' Nellie snorted. 'When my man was alive, I knew all his goings and comings. I'd never trust a man as far as I'd throw him.'

But my mother wouldn't budge, and at last Nellie got up with a sigh and went off to Maggie Cooney's house to see if she would do any better. After that she tried one house after another, until the whole island knew that something was afoot, though no one could make out what it was.

Because of Nellie's talk, everyone was out to see the men going down to the boats in the morning. It was a clean, windy day with a dark blue sea and long, high trailing clouds. Silently they hauled up sail. As they were about to cast off, my father saw the butt of the gun that Bartley kept for shooting seals, half hidden under a coil of rope. He put out his hand and took it, and handed it up to my mother, who was standing on the quay looking down into the boat. She took it awkwardly. Bartley said not a word. A gasp went up from the little crowd of watchers, then Nellie called out,

'Murder! That's what it is!'

The two boats slid away from the quay and set their course for the Island of Ghosts.

Chapter Fourteen

THROUGHOUT THE VOYAGE the men were very quiet, oppressed by the grim crowd of women that had seen them off and by Nellie Mór's words. The boats had to keep a distance from each other to allow room for movement, with my father's in the lead. It was too far to hear, but he knew that there was no laughing and singing going on in the other boat, as there would have been on any other expedition. The dark sea seemed to race past them and the wind blew them on as steadily as if they were in a fairy ship from the old times.

Bartley was at the tiller, and after a while my father went to him and said quietly,

'Your gun is gone. You have to forget your hatred now and think like a Christian.'

'He's no Christian,' Bartley said savagely. 'I'll need no gun. Haven't I my hands?'

'Remember your promise.'

'All right. But if that man puts a foot on Inishglass

again, it's all up with him.'

My father had to be satisfied with that. He had less to fear from the other men, since their children were not concerned, but still he went to each in turn and reminded him that there was to be no violence of any kind.

'I don't want to fight anyone,' Cumeen Peter said. 'But the less time we spend in that place the better.'

'I never thought I'd set foot on it at all,' Seán Black said.

As they came closer to the Island of Ghosts, both men looked more and more nervous. Cumeen said longingly,

'But look at the fine grass and the lovely high hill. It's a sin that we can never make use of it.'

'Someone is using it,' my father said. 'Look at the sheep grazing, and the goats.'

'There's some kind of a cove at the windward side,' Bartley said. 'I always heard that you could get moorings there in good weather.'

After that they were silent, as they steered a course around the tip of the island. Colie Joyce had brought his boat closer but he didn't call out for directions. All eyes were fixed on the rocky coastline, watching for an opening. When they saw it, Bartley steered in smoothly, followed by the second boat.

As my father said afterwards, they nearly wrecked

their own boats in their astonishment when they saw Mr Lennon's *gleoiteog* tied up neatly to a ring in the rock wall. His own heart went as cold as a stone. Why, if they had a good boat, had the girls not come home again? The only answer that came to him was that we had all died on the island.

The eight of them leaped ashore and raced up the hill towards the house, sea-boots thundering so that they sounded like a herd of wild horses. We heard them in the kitchen, where Bardal had just said we would all live forever on Hy-Breasail. They burst in through the doorway, eyes wild and staring, my father and Bartley in front, then the rest, crowding on top of one another. There was not room for all of them, so that some had to stay filling the doorway, peering in over each others' shoulders.

Barbara helped Brendan to the big chair by the fire and laid his crutches beside him on the floor. Cáit and I had backed away against the far wall, and stood there without moving, as if the men were enemies instead of rescuers.

There was a pause while they took in the scene, everyone staring at us and we staring back at them. We had reason to be nervous of them, since all four of us had sneaked off without by-your-leave. They had every right to be furious with us for the trouble we had caused. Then my father let out a hearty laugh.

'Safe and sound! Not a bother on them! Living the good life! Healthy as a school of fish – even the dog!'

'Not too healthy,' Bartley said, pointing to Brendan's crutch. 'What happened to you, *a mhic*?'

'I fell in the stream and broke my leg,' Brendan said. 'Mr Webb set it for me.'

The men all turned to stare at Bardal and I could see them clearly marking this up in his favour. He gazed back at them, his crazy blue eyes seeming to bore into them without expression. My father, who knew him better than anyone, sensed something of what was going on in his head. Bran moved close to me and crouched low, his eyes rolling from one face to the other.

'We've come to take them home, *a Bhardail*,' my father said quietly. 'You know they can't stay here forever. You can imagine the lamentations there were for them, first the boys and then the girls. The mothers are at home, heartbroken.'

'They can stay,' Mr Webb said raspingly. 'They live here now.'

Bartley took a threatening step forward, his fists clenched. My father moved quickly in front of him, blocking his way. Bardal's voice took on an even sharper tone, one we recognized only too well.

'They've lived here for six months. You said a moment ago that they're healthy and well, better than they've ever been in their lives, and yet you want to shut them up in boarding-schools where they'll have their heads filled with nonsense and their stomachs with all kinds of bad food.'

'You taught them for those scholarships yourself.'

'I did not. I taught them for the sake of knowledge. I've been teaching them here – isn't that so?'

He turned his gaze on me suddenly.

'Yes,' I mumbled. 'We've learned a great deal.'

'You see,' he said triumphantly. 'They've learned things they would never learn at school. I can show you. We haven't finished yet but we're well started on all kinds of works. We've built a dam for irrigation. We're going to have a turbine on the stream for electricity, to work our spinning and weaving machines. We'll be able to weave our own cloth. We make our own cheese already.'

'Have you some cows, then?' Colie Joyce asked eagerly.

'Sheep and goats, as healthy as the boys and girls.'

'We always heard that animals and children would die here.'

'Superstition, like the story of the ghosts,' Bardal said.

'Old stories. Not a word of truth in them.'

'The story of the ghosts is true,' I said after a moment. 'Brendan and I have both seen her. It's a woman in a long black skirt, with her hair in a bun. She doesn't speak but we hear a child crying.'

A long 'Whoo!' went up from the listening men. Some of those at the back moved out on to the paved path, where we could hear them talking excitedly among themselves. Bardal looked directly at me.

'So that's why you'll leave me,' he said. 'What does she matter? She died a long time ago. She should be pleased with our work.'

'You have seen her, then.'

'Yes.'

'And you don't care about her?'

'I can do nothing for her. What's the use of caring?'

'If I told you we could do something, would that change your mind?' my father asked.

'She died a long time ago,' he said again. 'I know what you're thinking of. Prayers – holy water –'

'Decent burial. Have you found her bones?'

I knew at once that he had. For the first time he dropped his eyes. When he lifted them again they seemed more remote than ever, looking into a distance that none of us could see.

'Some bones are never buried,' he said, almost as if he were talking to himself. 'Some plunge to the bottom of the sea and are never seen again. Some are lost in the jungle – what does decent burial mean?'

'Prayers, holy water, rest in peace.'

'Do that if you like,' he said contemptuously.

'Where are they?'

'Under the turf-rick. Take them if you want to.' With one of his quick movements, in a flash he had whipped out a small revolver from the breast pocket of his jacket. 'But if anyone tries to take away these young people, I'll shoot them all.'

'Put that gun away,' my father said quietly. 'We haven't finished talking yet.'

'I've finished. I've said my say. Now you had better go.'

Suddenly Brendan gave a wild yell and plunged forward, lifting his crutch high and smashing it down on Bardal's wrist so that the gun flew from his hand and shot across the floor. Instantly, my father and Bartley leaped forward and pinioned him by the arms. Colie picked up the little gun and examined it silently, turning it over and over in his hands. Brendan placed the crutch upright and limped with it back to his chair, where he sat with his head down, shaking all over.

They walked Bardal to his own chair at the head of the

table and made him sit down, and stood beside him with a hand each on his shoulders. It was a sad sight to see him conquered, though you'd think we should have been jumping with delight. At a nod from my father Colie went outside and we could hear him talking to the other men. Then they all went around to the end of the house where the turf-stack was.

None of us moved or spoke. Through the open door, for a while we could hear them throwing down the sods of turf, then nothing.

It seemed an age before Colie appeared in the doorway again, his huge head bowed so that we were barely able to see his face.

'We found her, Tomás, and the child with her,' he said. 'What are we to do now?'

'I don't know. If we could take them back to Inishglass, we could have a proper funeral for them when the priest comes.'

Mr Webb had been gazing down at his feet since his capture, the picture of defeat. Now he looked up suddenly and said, 'You don't have to do that. There's an old graveyard up on the hill, by the ruins of the cell.'

'What cell? What are you talking about? I never heard of a cell,' Bartley said sharply.

'That's all you know about your own island,' Mr Webb

said. 'Of course there's a cell where Saint Brendan founded a little monastery.'

'I've heard this used to be called Brendan's Island, right enough,' Bartley said, 'but that would have been in my grandfather's time.'

'If you want to see it, I can show you now. If you're afraid to let go of me,' he said mockingly, 'Dara will take you there.'

Now they were all looking at me.

'Have you seen it?' my father asked.

'There is a tiny field with pieces of headstones and the remains of a wall.'

I stopped there, suddenly realizing the meaning of that broken wall. On our islands, cells built soon after the arrival of Saint Patrick are still standing as good as new. In the back of my mind I had wondered why this one was so depleted. Now I realized that Bardal had of course removed the stones to build his extensions to this very house. The missing headstones would be his window-sills. He was watching me.

'That is the cell,' he said, and I felt that he was daring me to say any more about it.

I shut my mouth tightly, fearing they would kill him if they knew. Neither Brendan nor the girls had noticed anything.

'Then take us there,' my father said.

It was a sign of peace. The girls stayed with Brendan but I wanted to see the end of the business. The men took shovels from the tool-shed and within an hour they had laid the poor bones in the old graveyard. On his next visit to Inishglass, they said, the priest would be brought over to say the right prayers and the ghost would be laid forever. Mr Webb watched them silently as they worked, each man intent and reverent, each one dropping on one knee to say a prayer for the dead before shovelling in the last of the earth, as they would do at home.

I moved close to Bardal and said quietly,

'There's a tradition, in front of your nose. You're always talking to us about traditions and traditional living. How can you have respect for one tradition and not for another?'

I had intended to insult him but all he said was,

'So I've taught you to think.'

And he gave me his old familiar satirical look.

When they had finished, the men held a consultation. The burial had delayed them too long and they were anxious to get home at once.

'We'll have to take the children back to their mothers,' my father said. 'You know that, Bardal.'

'I know.'

'We could have the law on you, but we won't. They're safe and well.'

Bartley growled at this but the others quieted him. 'One thing I'd like to know,' Colie said. 'Did you destroy your own good boat on purpose, or was it the storm?'

'It was the storm.'

All the men looked relieved. I think they could have understood anything but that.

'And the other boat, the teacher's *gleoiteog*? Weren't you afraid they would sail off in that some fine morning without your leave?'

'No. I thought they would agree to stay. I thought they were beginning to see that they had a better chance here, and that they would never want to go home.'

'But you had heard on your radio that the whole world knew of the four young people that were drowned, first the boys and then the girls. Weren't you afraid the Army would come to look for them?'

'It was a nine days' wonder. Who remembers the sensations and the tragedies of last year?' Mr Webb said bitterly.

As we walked back to the house I said to him quietly, 'I must go home now but I'll come to visit you, after a while.'

'Why?' He sounded almost like his old, sour self.

'I like our life here. I'm an islandman all my life.'

'You're not a man at all yet.'

'It won't be long. I'll come back.'

I needn't describe our return home and the welcome we got, especially from the two mothers. I thought mine would pin me to her apron forever. Every time I went out of the house she stood at the door to see me go, and each time I came back I got a hero's welcome even if I had only been down to the potato-pit. Brendan's mother was the same, and Barbara and Cáit scarcely left their homes at all in the first few weeks.

My father had a hard job to persuade the men not to descend on the Island of Ghosts and burn out Mr Webb's house, in revenge for what he had done to us. They listened to him in the end, as they always did, especially when he got the priest on his side. There was a big day when all the boats went over for the blessing of the grave and the renaming of the island. Brendan's Island was its name from then on. That day, we had to stay at home.

Mr Lennon was there, however, sailing his own *gleoiteog*. He spent most of the day admiring the new works and in the evening he announced that he would return on my father's boat as he had given his own to Mr Webb.

'I don't use it much,' he said. 'That man is a genius. You can't leave a man like that without a boat.'

It was a good six months before I was able to persuade my father to take me back to the island. We went early one September morning and spent the day there. Mr Webb had seen us coming and was waiting at the harbour, and I could see that the two old friends were glad to be reunited. Almost at once Bardal said,

'Why hasn't this young man gone off to Galway to take up his scholarship?'

'He doesn't want to,' my father said. 'Brendan has gone but Dara says he would rather stay here with us.'

After that others came from time to time but no one wanted to stay there. I think they would never have learned to trust the place at all if Cáit and I hadn't gone there to live when we were married. That was years later. One person who would never come was Brendan. He and Barbara have the grassy farm in Tipperary that he always wanted, where they breed horses. When we go to visit them, we have to wait until he goes out of the room before we can answer her questions about Mr Webb, and about our life on Hy-Breasail.

Also by Eilís Dillon

THE HOUSE ON THE SHORE

Jim O'Malley has never met his wealthy Uncle Martin from Cloghanmore, so when he is sent to live and work with his uncle he is not sure what to expect. What he finds is an empty, run-down house and villagers whose welcome for him disappears at the mention of Martin's name. What has happened to his uncle? The arrival of the two strange foregin men is even more frightening – who are they and why are they looking for Uncle Martin? Jim resolves to find out what is going on, but he is not prepared for the truth ...

Paperback £4.99/€6.34/$7.95

THE LOST ISLAND

The lost island is a mystery. No one knows where it is – or whether it really exists. But everyone knows that some great reward is to be found there by anyone brave enough to seek it. Michael's father set out to find the lost island but he never returned. Now it is Michael's turn. He gets a boat and with his friend, Joe, sets off across unknown seas to try to discover the island's secret.

Paperback £4.99/€6.34/$7.95

FROM SIOBHÁN PARKINSON

FOUR KIDS, THREE CATS, TWO COWS, ONE WITCH (maybe)

Beverly, a bit of a snob, cooks up a plot to visit the island off the coast. She manages to convince the somewhat cautious Elizabeth and her slob of a brother, Gerard. A surprise companion is Kevin, the cool guy who works in the local shop. This motley crew must find ways to support each other and put up with one another's shortcomings, when they become stranded on the island and encounter a strange inhabitant.

Paperback £4.99/€6.34/$7.95

Send for our full colour catalogue